Alchemy

K J WIGNALL

Alchemy

First published in Great Britain in 2012
by Electric Monkey, an imprint of Egmont UK Limited
239 Kensington High Street
London W8 6SA

Text copyright © 2012 K J Wignall

The moral rights of the author have been asserted

ISBN 978 1 4052 5861 6

1 3 5 7 9 10 8 6 4 2

www.electricmonkeybooks.co.uk

A CIP catalogue record for this title is available from the British Library

Typeset by Avon DataSet Ltd, Bidford on Avon, Warwickshire

Printed and bound in Great Britain by the CPI Group

48092/1

EGMONT

Our story began over a century ago, when seventeen-year-old
Egmont Harald Petersen found a coin in the street. He was on
his way to buy a flyswatter, a small hand-operated printing
machine that he then set up in his tiny apartment.

The coin brought him such good luck that today Egmont has
offices in over 30 countries around the world. And that lucky
coin is still kept at the company's head offices in Denmark.

For B

1

A demon ended my childhood. The year was 1742 and I was just eight years old. I was not bitten, do not think that of me, but in a very real sense I was infected, and the darkness of that creature crept into my heart. It is lodged there still, and the only way I'll ever be free of it is to rid the world of the demon itself, and of the evil that comes with it.

I was born, then, in 1734, the youngest son of the fourth Lord Bowcastle. My father was a benign and generous man, inclined to view his two sons and two daughters in a spirit of wonder and benevolence. My mother, for the first eight years of my life, was spirited and beautiful and full of good humour. She kept the beauty thereafter, but the spirit of Lady Bowcastle, formerly Miss Arabella Harriman, only daughter of Sir Thomas and Lady Harriman, was broken beyond repair that night in 1742.

She'd accompanied my eldest sister, who'd just come out into society, to some happening or other in the city.

I remember the beginning of the evening well, not least as my final moment of undiluted happiness. I remember telling my sister how beautiful she looked. And my mother danced with me in the hall as they waited for the carriage to be brought around.

I was in bed by the time they returned and the next day I knew only that my mother was unwell. But in the days and weeks that followed, young as I was, I became my mother's confidant. The story within the house was that Lady Bowcastle had seen a spectre as she'd stepped down from her carriage, a wraith or some such thing. Only I was told the truth.

What my mother had seen that night was a demon, a demon that had haunted her youth. She had perhaps long consigned those youthful encounters to the deepest recesses of her mind, but seeing him again, completely unchanged after almost thirty years, was enough to bring it all to the surface and unsettle her well-being.

Had the demon not been there that night, or had she looked the other way and failed to see him, everything would have been different. Only he was there, and she did look and did see. It destroyed her health and changed the course of my life even before I knew it.

From that night forward, she determined that I would become the defender of her soul, that I would learn to understand such demons, this demon in particular, and that I would destroy them wherever I encountered them. She determined, young as I was, that I would become a champion for the cause of good.

And that, in short, is how I came to be the man I am: warrior, alchemist, sorcerer. My name is Phillip Wyndham and I have lived through a quarter of a millennium and more because of my mother's foresight and conviction, and because the demon itself still lives despite my promise that I would destroy it. The demon also has a name of course, and its name is William of Mercia.

2

The parkland was frozen, a thick hoar frost painting each branch white against the night sky. There had been no snow since the week after Christmas, but now, nearing the end of January, more was forecast to fall in the days ahead.

The weather made little difference to Will, but he was very conscious of how visible he was, a lone, dark figure crossing the frost-lit lawns as he made his way to what was now known as the 'old' house, Marland Abbey School. It loomed up in front of him, a jumble of Jacobean towers with cupola roofs and flagpoles, dotted with lit windows which seemed inviting even to him.

For the last few weeks, Will had been living in the cellars of the new house, a Gothic creation meant to recall the abbey, the ruins of which stretched away from the east lawns. Built in the nineteenth century, the new house had marked the beginning of the end for his brother Edward's descendants, the titles evaporating with an absence of sons, the estates with a series of foolish schemes and bad investments.

Now it was owned by the National Trust and run as a tourist attraction. It was closed for the winter, which made Will's residence easier, although he couldn't help but be filled with sadness that it was no longer home to his family, the Mercian Earls, the Dangraves – the Heston-Dangraves as they'd become after the titles had gone. Had this been the point of it all, to leave two beautiful buildings set in two hundred acres of parkland?

He stopped walking, having come as close to the school as he dared approach so early in the evening. He could see all he needed to anyway. From here he had a clear view through the windows of the Dangrave House common room – Eloise's house – and watched now as the students strolled in after dinner.

Eloise had told him Marland was a progressive school, offering more freedoms to students than was usual, and this showed itself in an odd way with their uniforms.

From a distance, they all appeared to be dressed alike, pale blue and white striped shirts without ties, all worn with the collars turned up for some reason, green jumpers, the boys in pale grey trousers. Some of the girls wore trousers too, while others, including Eloise, wore tartan skirts over pale grey tights. Will wasn't entirely sure where the Scottish connection came from.

On closer inspection though, the green jumpers varied in size and shape, all looking home-knitted, some of them cardigans rather than pullovers. It appeared to be the one element of the uniform through which the students were allowed to express their personalities, albeit in green. It added in some way to their relaxed and easy manner as they walked into the common room – there was no question that this was a privileged and comfortable existence. They flopped into armchairs and sofas or stood chatting in small groups full of laughter.

Will envied them, the warmth of their world, the companionship, the sense of belonging. He envied them most, of course, for the fleeting nature of the life they were leading right now. Good or bad, these intense heady schooldays would be over in the blink of an eye and would melt away as quickly as the frost beneath even the weakest winter sun.

These people in front of him, some looking younger, a few even looking older than Will, their lives would all move on. He'd failed to leave his own youth behind, so looked on longingly at that quality in the lives of others, cursing himself, wishing it might have been other than this.

And then his spirits lifted at the sight of the one thing that did give meaning to the last eight centuries of torment. Eloise walked into the room, deep in conversation with another girl. Eloise. The sight of her contented him and held his soul fast. She'd leave him behind too, but he didn't want to think of that now, he wanted only to watch and wait for her.

She crossed the room and sat on the arm of a chair, suggesting in her body language that she wouldn't be staying long. Then someone stood between her and the window, obscuring her from view, and Will spotted another student, Marcus Jenkins, the boy who'd joined the school at the beginning of term. His jumper, Will noted, looked suitably home-made, but fitted a little too well, marking him out as a new boy.

He was listening intently to other boys, but as if sensing Will's gaze, he turned and looked directly towards him. It unsettled Will, even though he knew the boy could only be staring at his own reflection in the window. There was something strange in the boy's bearing, stranger even than his sudden appearance here at Marland.

Will remembered him of course. At first he hadn't been able to place where he'd seen him before, but then he'd spotted the white ghost of a scar on Marcus's cheek and it had all come back to him – this was one of the boys who'd harassed Eloise that night by the river.

Briefly, Will wondered whether he would have come to know Eloise at all had it not been for rescuing her from those boys. But his memories fixed on Marcus again, whose name he had not then known, whose appearance was now so very different, and who'd been the only one of Taz's gang not to run in fear.

They hadn't encountered each other here at Marland, but Will had the feeling that Marcus Jenkins knew he was here, and that meant other people knew it too. Though Asmund had failed to mention it, though Jex's notebook hadn't referred to it, Marland seemed to hold the key to finding Lorcan Labraid and the truth of Will's destiny.

Marcus turned away and at the same time Will realised Eloise had left the common room. She would change before coming out to him, but he prayed for her to hurry. He could feel a familiar and sickly emptiness taking hold deep inside and he was certain her presence could keep it at bay.

But this wasn't the pining of a lovesick youth, this was his need for blood resurfacing, too soon after he'd fed from Jex. Of course, Jex had been no ordinary victim so it should hardly have been a surprise that the poor homeless man's youth and health had sustained Will for so short a time. A life stolen just two months before, and yet here were the first pangs of a spiritual hunger that would build over the days and weeks ahead until he could think of nothing else.

It was as if the changes taking place in his world were using up his energy more greedily. He'd come to know how much life was in a person's blood and how long it would last, even without understanding the 'why' or 'how' of it, but as with everything else, the rhythms he'd established over centuries now counted for nothing.

Was it because of the energy expended fighting Asmund – surely a battle to the death with the creature who'd infected him would have taken its toll – or combating the demons conjured up by Wyndham? Or was it something more fundamental – was everything speeding up now as Will gained speed himself, hurtling towards his own destiny?

He heard a door open somewhere nearby and instinctively stepped back, though the whitened lawns offered no immediate hiding place. Some of the teachers would occasionally come outside in the evenings to talk on their phones, and he didn't want one of them to alert the school to a possible prowler.

He needn't have worried though, and was perhaps less visible than he'd thought because he heard Eloise's uncertain and hushed voice call, "Will?"

"I'm here."

She changed course and came directly towards him. As she reached him, she smiled, but then looked concerned and put her hand on his arm as she said, "Are you OK?"

He watched her breath rising in a cloud of mist in the cold air, felt the warmth of her hand on his arm, the scent of her. It should have made his hunger worse, but as he'd hoped, her presence relaxed him.

He smiled and said, "I'm fine."

Even as he said it, he looked up at one of the darkened windows high above, sensing that someone was looking down at them. He glanced back at the lit window of the common room where Marcus was playing chess, studying the board – so at least it couldn't be him. But Will definitely felt they were being watched.

"Are you sure? You look . . ."

"Pale?" She laughed and he said, "Truly, I'm fine, but let's walk – I don't like being here so early in the evening."

She nodded and they set off across the lawns, two black-clad figures.

"You don't get unwell," said Eloise as they walked. "But you did look unwell, just now."

"I could argue that I've been unwell for a very long time. But you shouldn't worry – it's something that comes and goes, something I'm familiar with."

"But . . ." Eloise didn't stop walking because, he assumed, it was so cold out here as to discourage standing still, but the mental leap she'd just made required some physical response and she clutched his arm as she said, "It can't be! You need blood? But you said Jex's blood would last a long time."

Will put his hand on hers in an attempt to offer reassurance, but she slipped her hand out from under his in response. Perhaps it was a direct reaction to the coldness of his touch, or perhaps revulsion because this had reminded her of what he really was. He could hardly blame her for rejecting him.

"I thought it would, and I cannot understand why it hasn't." He walked a few paces in silence. Their footsteps crunched softly on the frozen grass. "But I'm glad of it in one sense. It allows you to see and understand what I have told you many times, that I'm a monster. It's no longer just a homeless man who died before I met you. I will have to kill somebody. For the moment I can withstand it, but within weeks the need will become so bad that even you would not be safe – you saw the way Asmund had become."

At first he thought Eloise might not respond, but then she said, "How soon?"

"As soon as I find someone suitable. I may need to spend a night or two in the city, at least within the next two weeks."

"There's no other way?" She was hopeful, even

11

though she knew the answer. Then she said, "Promise me you'll . . ." But that line of thought also dried up.

"Eloise, there is no way to justify this. I pick people who won't be missed, people who have slipped through the cracks of society, but two months ago that could easily have been you. No life is worth so little as to excuse my taking it."

"But you're not a monster, and I'm sorry, I didn't mean to pull my hand away – it was the shock of how cold you are out here, that's all."

"Am I very cold?"

She nodded, giving a small, almost regretful smile. "I don't want you to kill anyone else. I know you have to, but I don't want you to, so maybe that's just a sign that we have to move faster. The more we learn, the more we find out why this happened to you, the more chance we have of . . . breaking the cycle, I suppose."

Will smiled back at her, touched by her innocent optimism, as if she felt he might be cured in some way. Briefly, that thought planted a seed of optimism in his own soul, but he knew there could be no cure for this disease, except perhaps the one that Wyndham wanted for him.

They passed around the edge of a small plantation of trees, designed to screen one house from the other, then started towards the desolate shadows of the new house.

At the sight of it, Will said, "I'm glad we've talked about this, but it completely distracted me from what I had to tell you. I've made a discovery."

This time Eloise did stop walking as she said, "So have I! But yours first. What have you found?"

"A tunnel. Or tunnels, and I'm certain they lead under the old abbey."

"From where?"

He pointed as he said, "From the house."

They walked on, but Eloise said, "I don't get it – you've searched the cellars again and again."

"True, and I was determined I would find something. I have half a memory from my childhood visits here, talk of tunnels underground, tunnels that long predated the abbey itself. And I know too that if Asmund's master or even Lorcan Labraid himself is here at Marland, he must be underground. That's why I kept searching."

"I don't get it – underground, but not in the cellars?"

"The cellars would be too obvious perhaps. A passage leads down from the house itself, rather fittingly from the library – we always seem to return to books."

Eloise knew that Will stayed in the cellars during the day and so she said, "Did you find them last night, or – surely not this evening?"

"Just this evening. I haven't even explored them myself. I found them and came directly to meet you."

She looked pleased by that, knowing that they would explore the tunnels together for the first time. And that in itself sparked misgivings in his own mind. He could no longer deny Eloise's part in this, but he realised he should have searched the tunnels on his own first. As it was, he had no idea what he was about to lead her into.

3

Once inside the house, Will took Eloise by the hand and led her through the unlit rooms to the library – there was unlikely to be anyone for miles around who might see lights on in the house, but it was still safer to leave it in darkness. Eloise couldn't see a thing, but walked confidently, trusting him entirely.

When they reached the library, he opened the wooden panel in the wall that led to the first secret passage, and once they were inside he put on his dark glasses and turned on the light. Eloise blinked against the brightness at first, but adjusted quickly and looked around the small narrow room in which they found themselves; it was bare-walled, with a metal spiral staircase leading up to the next floor.

Will saw her confusion and said, "The trustees know about this secret passage. During my hours of confinement in the cellar I've read all the literature offered in the shop." Even as he said it, he found it extraordinary that his family's great house had been reduced to having a

15

gift shop for souvenir-hungry tourists. "It's mentioned that Thomas Heston-Dangrave built a secret passage – fashionable at the time – to link the library with the master bedroom. It says nothing else."

Eloise looked at the walls and said, "There is nothing else."

Will nodded. "So it appears, but I was standing with my hands resting on this wall, thinking, wondering what it was that I was looking for, when this happened."

He reached up and put his palms flat on the wall and almost immediately felt the mechanism that lay deep within the stones grinding into life. With surprising speed, the wall trundled sideways, exposing a set of stone steps that disappeared into the darkness below.

He'd been no further than this himself yet, but he could tell from the air that these steps led to something extensive. He stepped back for Eloise to see, but she was still staring at the space into which the wall had slid.

"How did you do that?"

"I don't know. I can only presume it's the same power I have over locks and other such things – after all, the wall must contain a mechanism and I assume somewhere there's a device for opening it, though I don't know where."

"At least there's a light switch," said Eloise, pointing to the wall at the top of the steps. She turned it on and lights appeared at regular intervals, illuminating the descent in front of them.

Will hadn't noticed the switch earlier and was a little disappointed because it meant someone in modern times had at least partially explored whatever network lay below. Somehow, it made it less likely that Lorcan Labraid would be found there – Will doubted that the evil of the world would have permitted workmen to install electric cables.

He looked at the switch and said, "From the 1920s, I would say." The disappointment receded, replaced by another thought. "Thomas Heston-Dangrave knew about these tunnels – he incorporated them into the design of the house he built. If my guess is right about the age of this switch, his great-great-grandson George also knew about them because he must have installed the lights. Perhaps his own daughters knew too, but those two spinsters must have taken the secret to the grave with them."

"Of course. Otherwise the National Trust would have made something of it. And if the family kept it to themselves, we have to assume there was some reason for doing so."

Had they kept it hidden, wondered Will, because these tunnels spoke of secrets, of a secret shared history between his family and this place. If so, he was certain

17

it predated the family's acquisition of these lands during the dissolution of the monasteries.

He wished he could recall more than the fragments of memories he had of Marland. Even in those weeks before his sickness, he'd been aware of Marland's importance to his father and perhaps, if he'd lived longer, that bond would have been explained to him. Perhaps it had been explained to his brother Edward once he was grown and yet it was to Will that it truly mattered.

Will looked at Eloise and said, "Shall we?"

He took the steps first and she followed close behind. But as he neared the bottom and the sense of space and air stretching away from them became greater, he regretted that he'd come here without any form of weapon. For all he knew there could be another like Asmund down here, or demons the like of which he hadn't yet encountered.

As he'd expected, at the bottom the passageway turned to the left and went on in a straight line for some way. By the time they reached the first junction with a choice of turning left or right, Will reckoned they were under the ruins of the abbey itself.

But they immediately noticed a change here. The first tunnel they'd walked along was perhaps a newer construction, built specifically by Thomas Heston-Dangrave to connect the house with this subterranean complex, for they were on the threshold now of something much older, and much more disturbing.

The walls here were covered with runic writing and other symbols, and a strange menagerie of monsters and demons, all engraved into the stone and painted in garish colours which had hardly faded over the centuries.

Eloise said, "Oh my God, this is incredible." She stepped forward, poring over the images and scripts on the wall in front of her, looking away only to check what Will had already spotted, that every part of the walls in every direction was similarly decorated. "This must've taken years." She continued to stare intently at the paintings in front of her.

Will couldn't quite share in her excitement. The lights also extended in both directions, so these tunnels had been navigated by workmen in the last hundred years, presumably in safety. But there was no disguising the fact that this was a strange and sinister place. Even if nothing had happened to them, he had little doubt that those workmen would have been keen to leave at the end of each day.

There was something untamed and primal here. The very stones seemed to breathe and murmur as if possessed of some form of life, and though there was nothing living close by, Will had an acute sense that they were not entirely alone either.

He saw Eloise shudder and she turned and gave him a relieved smile, as if she'd feared for a moment that he'd left her there.

He smiled back and said, "Do you sense anything strange in the atmosphere down here?"

She still found it hard to take her eyes off the sinister richness of the walls but said, "Do you mean like, is my spine ice-cold, or are the hairs on the back of my neck standing up, or do I have a constant sense that someone's standing behind me? Because the answer is yes to all of the above."

"Really?"

"Really. I mean, this is amazing, but there's something unbelievably creepy about the place."

He nodded, looking along the tunnel in both directions, then turned to her again and said, "You know I won't let anything happen to you."

She looked bemused and said, "Put it this way, I wouldn't be here without you."

"Good. Then let's explore."

He gestured to the right and they walked along the tunnel for some way before turning left, through a short connecting passage to a parallel tunnel. It became clear soon enough that even though it doubled back on itself in places and led to dead ends, it was a massive circular network, drawing them slowly towards the centre.

And the closer they got to that centre, the feeling of some malevolent presence became all the more intense. Even the air was oppressive, the walls themselves possessed, as if a constant murmuring of ancient incantations was emerging from them just below the level of their hearing.

They walked passage after passage, turning corners, working inwards, and each time they turned, Will expected to be met by some creature or apparition. Yet there was only the empty tunnel with its subdued lights, receding into the gloom. But that didn't stop him expecting to meet something, didn't stop his increasing concern that he shouldn't have brought Eloise here until he'd explored these tunnels himself.

Despite her unease, Eloise seemed less concerned than Will, and rather than look ahead, she was transfixed by the walls, so vivid that they looked in places as if the artists had only recently left off their work. Her faith in Will was total, so much so that it didn't seem to occur to her that he might be out of his depth too.

Eventually they turned into a passage that curved and then delivered them into a small pentagonal chamber. The chamber had four other passages leading off it, but for some reason, one of those four exits led into darkness. Will's eyes were drawn automatically to that dark tunnel, but his attention was pulled away by Eloise.

"There are no decorations in here." It was true; the walls of this chamber were bare. "Oh, except for this."

Will followed her to the centre of the chamber. Embedded flat into the floor were four swords, their hilts outermost, their points meeting in the middle around a large medallion. All five pieces appeared to be cast in bronze. They looked down at the plate-sized medallion, the relief on its surface as clearly visible as if it had been cast that morning.

"Oh my God," said Eloise. She dropped to her knees to look closer and said, "What do you think it means?"

"I don't know," said Will and looked round the chamber. He saw now that the walls were not completely bare, that in four places, following the line of the swords out past their hilts to the walls, were brief inscriptions in the same runic writing that was to be found everywhere else. "There are four inscriptions on the walls, perhaps names, perhaps each relating to one of the swords. The swords could represent people."

Eloise looked up at him, slightly exasperated as she said, "But what about this, Will?"

He looked again at the circular bronze relief, the four sword tips almost appearing to hold it in place. It was the boar's head, his family's crest, and a larger but identical version of the broken medallion they wore between them.

"I don't know. Except that in some way it confirms we're looking in the right place."

As he spoke, he felt a slight breeze brush across his face and turned to look at the darkened tunnel. It had come from there, he was certain of it. Eloise had felt it too and stood again.

"A breeze – that means it leads to the open air, doesn't it?"

"Not necessarily." Will took a couple of steps forward, into the mouth of the passageway, and once away from the lights of the chamber, he could see some way along it. There was nothing different about it, the same abundance of decoration. And in fact, he could see light fittings dotted along it in much the same way.

"There are light fittings here too. I think they've fused, no more than that." Yet now, for the first time since they'd entered the tunnels, Will actually felt the hairs rise on his neck, a shiver running through him. There was something there, beyond the edge of even his night vision, and it was something he did not want to face, not now, not without weapons, not with Eloise.

He stepped backwards into the chamber and tried to look casual while keeping an eye on the darkened tunnel. Eloise didn't seem suspicious and was staring at the pattern of bronzes in the floor.

"I've seen this before somewhere. I wish I could remember where, but I know I've seen it."

"You don't just mean the medallion?"

"No, I mean the pattern, the circle in the middle, the four swords surrounding it, forming a sort of cross."

"Of course, now that you mention it, it is a cross – perhaps that's why it's familiar." Once again Will felt his eyes drawn to the darkness of the tunnel. There seemed no immediate threat, nothing he could hear or smell, and yet something about it was disturbing him.

"No, it's not the cross." She looked up and smiled. "Don't worry, it'll come to me."

Will nodded, but said, "I think we should stop for this evening."

"But it's still early." Eloise looked at her watch. "Oh. I can't believe we've been down here an hour. *And* we have to get back."

"It won't take us an hour to get back, but we should go. And you still haven't told me your discovery." As he spoke, he gestured for her to lead the way out, not wanting to leave her behind in the chamber, with that darkness and whatever it concealed. And he looked back a couple of times as they walked away, still expecting to see someone, or something, appearing out of the shadows.

Eloise walked on, sensing none of his greater unease

as she said, "Of course, I'd completely forgotten." She waited until he was alongside her and said, "I found out who's paying Marcus Jenkins' fees." She responded to Will's look of surprise by saying, "Don't worry, I haven't been playing the detective – I just overheard him mentioning it to the boy he plays chess with, then researched it online. His fees are being paid by something called The Breakstorm Trust, and guess who one of the trustees is? Someone called Phillip Wyndham! OK, it's possible it's not our Wyndham, but . . ."

The news hit Will hard, not because it confirmed that Marcus Jenkins had come here as Wyndham's spy – that much he had never doubted – but because it spoke of another betrayal he'd suspected almost from the start.

"Oh, I have a feeling it's the same Wyndham. What time is it?"

"Nearly nine."

"Good, there's still time. I need to go back into the city tonight."

"Then I'll come with you. We can call Rachel and Chris and ask them . . ."

"No. It's a risk, but we'll call a taxi and ask it to collect us from here. There's a telephone here and I have money."

"But it'll take the taxi as long to get here as Rachel

and . . ." Eloise stopped herself and said, "How do you have money?"

Will was bemused by the odd things she found exceptional about his life when she so readily accepted all the true strangeness that surrounded him.

"Money comes to me here and there, and what belongs to the cathedral belongs to me – I give back whatever I have to the church each time I return to the earth."

"OK. But why do you want to take a taxi?"

"I want to surprise them. There might be a rational explanation, but I want to surprise them nevertheless. I saw brochures and leaflets from The Breakstorm Trust at Chris and Rachel's house, addressed to Chris. It was one of the occasions when I saw the spirits of the witches, and one of the leaflets blew to the floor – I should have known it was significant."

"Oh God, this isn't good. You felt weird about them the first time we went to The Whole Earth – I should have listened!" Eloise sounded distraught, fearing the same as Will, that Chris and Rachel had betrayed them, clearly upset too at the thought that she had been their defender against Will's suspicions. "But look, they're rich, and it's an educational charity, so they're absolutely the kind of people who'd be approached to donate."

"True. And they did have good reason to act oddly around me."

She looked confused for a moment, then the penny dropped and she said, "You mean filming you all those years ago?"

He thought of the middle-aged Arabella, collapsing at the sight of him, and set against that memory, Chris and Rachel's behaviour had been much more reasonable.

But he smiled, saying, "Yes, that's what I mean. It also has to be said that I couldn't have reached Asmund without them."

"And they've helped us so much these last couple of months. I mean, it would have been difficult getting you out here without them."

"Also true," said Will again, while equally aware that it possibly suited Wyndham to have Will come here, that perhaps his intention was not only to destroy Will, but also Lorcan Labraid, to unravel everything that had been woven together here over a thousand years and more.

They walked in silence for a short while and finally Eloise said, "What will you do if he has betrayed us?"

It was an interesting choice of words, he thought. As much as she didn't want to believe, she was already subconsciously deciding who the guilty party must be, suggesting it would be Chris rather than he and Rachel together who'd been treacherous. Yet on the other hand,

Eloise didn't believe it was just Will who might have been betrayed, but both of them, both of their destinies, and in that perhaps she was right.

"What am I to do? In my own time the answer would have been obvious, but now? Perhaps, as you suggest, we should hope for a credible explanation."

And Will hoped against hope that there would be one, because if there wasn't, he couldn't see how he could allow them to live, posing an ever greater danger to him. A spy was one thing, but if Chris and Rachel had betrayed him, he would have no choice but to kill them, and in so doing, he feared he'd also kill everything that existed between him and Eloise.

4

Eloise had doubted the taxi would come – she'd assumed the cab company, getting a call from a teenager asking for a car to come twenty minutes out of the city, would mark it down as a hoax. Maybe it was something in Will's tone of voice, some remnant of his former life, but Eloise's doubts proved unfounded, the booking was accepted and the taxi came. When asked to give a surname, he hadn't hesitated in saying "Wyndham" though he wasn't sure why.

As the car left Marland, the driver said, "What on earth were you doing out here at this time of night? It's closed in the winter."

Eloise looked alarmed, but Will said simply, "We'd prefer not to talk, if you don't mind."

"Fair enough," said the driver and turned the radio a little louder.

Eloise looked both shocked and amused that Will had spoken to him like that. But of course, the way she saw it, he was a young person speaking to an adult. As far as Will was concerned, he was a noble speaking to an inferior, someone being paid to carry out a simple service.

They travelled in silence. Will was thinking of the situation that lay ahead of them, and after ten minutes, Eloise gave away the fact that she was thinking about the same thing.

Unprompted, she said, "There has to be an explanation."

He nodded and no more was said, and then, as they travelled on into the suburban edges of the city, he found himself dreaming. He was walking as he had been several times before, among ruins on a sunny day. Someone called his name, but in an odd form, "William Dangrave?", a surname that he predated by more than a century, and he turned and saw Eloise, beautiful, luminous.

"I'm William Dangrave," he said, and stirred from the dream, nervous for a moment that he'd said those words aloud.

But the driver was staring intently at the road which looked icy here and there in front of them, and Eloise was sitting quietly next to Will. At some point in the last few minutes she'd slipped her hand into his. The warmth of her ran through him, seeming almost to fill him, and he clasped his fingers round hers.

She smiled at him, as if this simple act had been meant

to offer her reassurance, and he smiled back, though he knew that right now he could assure her of nothing.

They had the taxi drop them in a side street close to the city centre. Will paid the driver in full and told him to keep the change, but once Eloise was out of the car, he said, "Just a second." He opened the passenger door and climbed back in.

The taxi driver looked hostile. "What do you think you're doing? We're . . ." His eyes caught Will's and his words disappeared somewhere in his throat. The radio, which had been blaring some jangly and infectious tune, became a wall of static and frequency noise.

"Do you remember this evening? You collected an elderly man and woman, Mr and Mrs Wyndham. They'd been walking out at Marland. Their son's car broke down so they called a taxi to bring them back into the city. You were the driver of that taxi. Do you remember?" The driver offered a confused nod, lost in a dream of his own, and Will said finally, "Forget about us." He climbed back out of the car and closed the door.

Will and Eloise started to walk towards The Whole Earth and Eloise checked her watch and said, "Twenty to eleven, a good time to catch them." Then, as an afterthought, "You'll be able to get me back into school, won't you?"

"Of course."

"And you just got back into the taxi because . . .?" She looked behind and Will followed suit – the taxi driver was sitting where they'd left him, looking confused, fiddling with the buttons on his radio.

"I hypnotised him, muddied his thoughts – he'll have some vague recollection of us, but jumbled up with other things, false memories. The fewer people who remember us the better."

Eloise shook her head and said, "There are times when I realise I hardly know you at all. I mean, I know you, but I forget all the weird stuff."

"That's one of the reasons I like being with you."

She looked at Will questioningly.

"Because you make *me* forget the weird stuff. Sometimes when I'm with you I forget . . ." He tried to sum up the enormity of how transformed he was by her company, but he couldn't. "I just forget."

"Me too." She smiled, and they turned into the narrow street where The Whole Earth was located, less busy than usual, no doubt because of the cold. They were nearly at the café when Eloise said, "If there is a problem with Chris and Rachel, couldn't you hypnotise them to forget? Marcus Jenkins too."

"It would make life simpler, but I don't think so. For one thing, I imagine Wyndham is powerful enough to counter my limited efforts, perhaps even to use them against me. We should hope, instead, for simple explanations."

He stopped at the café door and Eloise stepped in ahead of him. Before Will was inside, he heard Rachel say, "This is a nice surprise! What are you doing here?"

Without missing a beat, Eloise said, "We needed to come into the city, but we wouldn't have asked you to fetch us during opening hours."

Rachel smiled and kissed Eloise on the cheek. She looked at Will, falling short of encroaching on his physical space, as she said, "Thanks. It *has* been manic this evening. Do you want to go through and we'll follow as soon as we're free."

Chris emerged from the kitchen carrying a tray with soup and bread on it. He looked visibly shocked at the sight of them standing there and it took a moment for him to regain his composure. He placed the food in front of a customer at a corner table, and by the time he turned back to them, he was smiling.

He approached with his arm outstretched, shaking Will's hand, then kissing Eloise on the cheek as Rachel had. Will noticed his hand was dry and hot, without the supposed tell-tale clamminess of the guilty.

"You didn't tell us you were coming in."

"They didn't want to call us away from the café," said Rachel. "Isn't that sweet of them?"

Her response was genuine, but it appeared to irritate Chris in some way, as if she'd broken his momentum. If that was the case, he rebounded quickly enough, saying, "Well, to be honest, this evening would've been difficult, but we'll take you back of course."

Someone called him from behind and he made his excuses and returned to work. Will and Eloise left Rachel and walked through to the house, sitting on the green sofas where Will had first confronted them about their interest in him. There was a sickly familiarity about the return of his suspicions, made worse by the realisation that Rachel and Chris had been privy to almost all his plans and movements these last two months.

They sat for a while in silence, listening to the distant sounds of the café winding down for the evening. Then Eloise looked at the bookshelves and said, "Do you think we'll ever see the spirits again?"

"You mean the witches?" She nodded. "Perhaps not. Perhaps they told us all they wished to impart. At least we know we have nothing to fear from them if they do return."

"I was just thinking, since Puckhurst nothing has actually . . . happened. I know we've just found the tunnels, but I thought things would keep happening, that we'd set something in motion."

Whether she knew she was doing it or not, she

played with the pendant hanging round her neck as she spoke. She was right, of course. If this was the time of his destiny, where was it, and why had the messengers failed to show themselves? Lorcan Labraid was calling to him, that was the essence of everything he'd learned in November, and yet now he was met with silence, scrabbling forward on his own, understanding nothing of what he'd so far found.

He thought of that darkened passageway in the tunnels though, and even here in the safety of the city it chilled his spine. The witches would be a welcome sight now, if only that he might ask them about those tunnels, that one tunnel in particular.

Eloise wanted something to happen, a desire he appreciated, yet still he said, "You know that old saying – be careful what you wish for."

As his words died away, Chris and Rachel came through from the café and Rachel said, "Can I get you anything, Eloise?"

"No thanks."

Chris said, "How is it being back at school?"

Eloise looked at him with a bemused expression, eyebrows raised, as if asking if he really needed a response to that question. Will often forgot that she was sixteen, over seven hundred and fifty years younger than him, but right then, she looked very much a schoolgirl.

"Please sit down," said Will. Eloise recognised his tone and suddenly looked adult again, nervous as to where this might lead. "I'll get straight to the point because I'm sure there's an explanation, and if there is, we can perhaps use it to our advantage."

"This sounds intriguing," said Chris as he and Rachel sat on the sofa opposite Will and Eloise.

"A pupil arrived at the school at the beginning of this term and for various reasons – not important at this moment – we're convinced that he's been placed there to spy on Eloise, and perhaps on me."

Rachel said, "But no one knows you're there."

She was innocent at least. Will could see it in her eyes, hear it in her voice.

"So we thought. Eloise found out who's paying this boy's fees and it's a charity called The Breakstorm Trust. You're involved with them, aren't you, Chris? I saw their brochures here last November, addressed to you."

Chris nodded, glancing at Rachel as he said, "We both donate to different charities. Breakstorm is an educational charity – I've given them money, that's about it." Rachel looked as if she was about to remind him of something, but he jumped in quickly as if offering the information voluntarily. "Oh, and I attended a dinner for donors."

36

"Where you would have met the trustees, including one Phillip Wyndham."

Chris laughed a little to himself, bitterly, with the look of someone disappointed that he'd let it come to this, then said, "Yes, I met Phillip Wyndham. In fact, I met him a couple of times, when he was outlining the work they did, discussing my donation."

Rachel looked astounded and said to Will, "Phillip Wyndham? The Wyndham who's trying to destroy you?"

"No," said Chris. "No, this can't be the same man. That's why I didn't mention it because I knew you'd find it suspicious and because I knew this couldn't be the same person. He's a suit, you know, a guy in his fifties who's been in business . . ."

"What business?"

"I don't know, but trust me, this guy is no sorcerer, he just isn't."

Eloise cleared her throat and said, "After we got back from Puckhurst, when we were sitting at the kitchen table, you actually brought the subject up – you asked who Wyndham was, how he fitted into things."

Chris nodded. "Because I'd done a check on Wyndham, just to be sure, and . . ."

"And?" Rachel looked as much in need of an answer as Will or Eloise.

"And I couldn't find any trace of him, except for Breakstorm itself. That doesn't mean there's anything suspicious about him – lots of rich and powerful people are hard to trace – but I asked that night because I suppose I wanted a little more reassurance."

No one spoke. Will was unsure what to think. Chris sounded like a person who was genuinely conflicted, finding it hard to believe the man he'd met could be the sorcerer trying to destroy Will. He also sounded desperate, but that said nothing of his guilt or innocence.

Finally Chris looked at Will, as if asking for a response.

Will said, "Tell me about the person you've met – Phillip Wyndham. What's he like? What does he talk about? Everything you can remember."

"Like I said, he's probably in his fifties, could be older or younger, but he's grey-haired, in pretty good shape, always very smartly dressed, the bearing of someone who's been a powerful businessman, though he's never talked about his past to me. He talked about education for the most part, a few polite questions about our business, about why we decided to open a café. He knew I was interested in the occult so he asked about that. But he didn't actually seem interested himself – he was humouring me, that was all."

Eloise said, "He didn't ask about Will in any way, not even . . . I don't know, sort of, leading questions?"

"No, that's my point exactly. That's why I can't believe he's the same person."

Rachel had been frowning as she listened. "But you should have told us, or at least me. You must see how it looks coming out like this."

Chris nodded and put his hand on Rachel's, but she pulled hers away, reminding Will of Eloise's gesture in the frozen parkland earlier. Was Rachel having a similar moment, wondering who this man was who was sharing her life?

"I didn't tell anyone because I thought you'd cut me out of everything, and I was certain there couldn't be a connection. Almost certain. But I should have told you all, and I apologise. I can try to find out more about him, but if you met him, you'd be as certain as I am that he has nothing to do with this."

Will smiled, trying to believe that Chris was just incredibly naïve, and said, "He is a leading trustee of a charity that quite inexplicably placed a boy in Eloise's school just as we returned there, a boy we do not doubt is a spy, and his surname is Wyndham. Do you not see, even if he isn't the sorcerer – the sorcerer, let me remind you, who conjured my own brother from his grave in order to attack me – he is at the very least a relative or accomplice of that person?"

"Of course, when you put it like that."

"Is there any other way of putting it?"

"No. I can't believe I've been so stupid," said Chris, and covered his face with his hands for a moment. When he took his hands away again, he looked determined. "You won't be able to trust me after this, obviously, so I can have no more direct involvement. Tell me nothing of your plans or what you've discovered. It's the only way you can be sure."

Will stared directly into his eyes, but didn't try to hook him in, wanting his answer to be completely uninfluenced, and said, "Have you betrayed me?"

"No, I swear on my life."

"And I will hold you to that. But if you have given your word, I'll accept it and we'll speak no more of it. You will be as privy to our plans as you were before. The only thing I can ask of you is that you respond with caution if you're contacted by Wyndham again."

"Of course, and I'll tell you, but I haven't heard from him in months, since around the time we met you."

"Good."

There was another awkward pause, but then Rachel smiled, trying to draw a line under the discussion by saying, "So how are things going?"

"Still nothing happening," said Eloise. "It's really annoying actually, specially after me going back to Marland."

"But we do have hopes of the school chapel and its crypt," said Will and Chris gave him a small grateful smile. "It's too soon to say if we'll discover anything specific, but it makes sense that the chapel of the old house should be significant."

Rachel looked up at the clock and said, "You won't be going there now though? It's late. I mean, Eloise, how are you managing to get up in the mornings?"

Eloise laughed and said, "I'm doing OK, and no, we're done for the night, but I suppose we'd better be going."

"Yes, if you don't mind."

Both Rachel and Chris accompanied them on the journey back, the conversation touching on the weather and Eloise's studies and anything else that would put some distance between the four of them and the suspicions and accusations that had been so recently aired.

They dropped them at the school gates to avoid suspicion, and Will and Eloise started walking up the long drive, sheltered from view by the woodland on both sides.

As soon as the car had gone, Eloise said, "I don't trust him."

Will laughed and said, "That's an interesting development."

She laughed too, but said, "Clearly, I'm not alone –

41

otherwise you wouldn't have made up all that business about the school chapel. Quick thinking."

"Thank you. But to answer your point, I'm not sure whether I trust him or not. Perhaps giving him that misinformation will lead us in due course to an answer."

A small branch snapped in the woods ahead of them. It wasn't unusual, but they were cautious and both stopped walking and listened. After a moment, Eloise whispered, "Can you see anyone?"

Will couldn't, and in fact the hoar frost would have made it hard for someone to hide even from regular eyes, let alone his.

"No, I don't think there's anyone there." But he didn't move and nor did Eloise.

Now that they'd been alerted by that snapping twig, they were both aware that something was not as it should be. Will could still hear Chris and Rachel's car disappearing into the far distance, he could hear the hissing release of steam from the school boiler, Eloise's breathing, but he could hear something else too, something faint and disturbing.

A moment later, Eloise said, "What's that noise? I can hear something." She looked up, her breath rising above her.

Will looked too, and could hear the sound more clearly now, like a sickening heartbeat, pumping, growing louder, and then he could see something. He couldn't make out what it was or how big because he couldn't tell how far away it was, but something, a darker shadow against the dark sky, was flying fast towards them.

5

Eloise cocked her head to one side and said, "It sounds like . . ."

"Wings," said Will. Not a heartbeat, but the beat of a wing, and guessing now that the dark shape was a bird, he was able to judge how close it was as it swooped in, aiming directly for Eloise's head.

Dark against darkness, hurtling, and silent now as even the wings stopped. Will lunged forward, moving fast. Eloise let out a confused cry, but it was already done. Will snatched the bird out of the air as it neared the end of its dive. He felt it break in his hand with the impact. He looked at it, there in his fist like a broken umbrella.

"A crow?" Eloise sounded astonished more than afraid.

Will nodded, but before he could speak, he heard the same beating sound. He dropped the dead bird and looked around, trying to see where the other one was. It came swooping down from behind them.

"Run," he said to Eloise. She hesitated and he pushed behind her and grabbed the bird out of the air. But the sound of beating wings didn't stop. Eloise let out a cry and when he turned she'd been scratched on the head and was hitting another crow away, the bird flying back beyond arm's reach before mounting another ferocious attack.

Will lashed out, knocking the crow into the trees at the side of the drive. And yet still he could hear more wingbeats in the air above them, and increasingly, the cawing of twenty, fifty, maybe even a hundred crows. They were ignoring him and it was clear that Eloise alone was their target.

He looked at her. The attack had left a small scratch at the top of her forehead, a bright patch of blood shining glossily in the midst of her pale skin. He felt the emptiness surge up inside him, the need to take in what that blood offered him.

But a shape swooped down from the dizzying carousel of shadows that was above and all around them. He hit out at the bird, its lifeless and broken body immediately falling to the ground a few paces away from them. And swiftly he removed his coat and threw it over Eloise's head, as much to conceal the blood from his view as to protect her.

"Keep that over your head and follow me." He took

her hand and led her forward quickly, fighting off the crows which attacked relentlessly now, some swooping low, but staying just out of reach, others diving straight for her. They remained blind to Will, even as he knocked them out of the air.

Eloise let out another scream and he stopped and saw that he'd missed one. It stabbed at her head through his coat, its beak hammering at her skull, determined. He knocked it away, but even as he did, three more swept in, grappling at her coat, pecking furiously.

He stopped trying to lead her forward and concentrated on defending her, knocking the birds out of the air, grabbing them when he could. But there were too many, and those he didn't kill swept in again relentlessly. He couldn't protect all directions at once, fearing even he would be overwhelmed.

Finally he realised there was only one option, to get Eloise inside. He started to pull her forward again, knocking the crows away when he could, reacting to her cries when they got through and clawed and pecked at her through the thick overcoat.

Then they reached the point where the woodland stopped and the drive curved round across the open parkland to the school, and as suddenly as the attack had started, so it stopped. One last crow, bigger than all the others, swept across the air in front of them, then arced up into the night sky and away.

Will and Eloise came to a halt. He could still hear the wingbeats high above, though the cawing had stopped now. And gradually the sound of the birds grew more and more distant. Eloise pulled his coat free and handed it back.

The coat had apparently saved her from any further injury, though she frowned as she rubbed her head. The wound on her forehead had also stopped bleeding in the cold air, but the blood still made Will almost light-headed with longing.

She realised immediately what was troubling him and said, "Sorry." She stepped back and took a tissue from her pocket and held it over the wound.

"It's not your fault, but you're right, it's better that you cover it."

He put his coat back on.

Eloise looked around. "What, I mean, *what* was that all about?"

Will looked back at the drive, littered with the bodies of birds, and said, "Let's get inside first – it serves no purpose to discuss it out here."

They walked swiftly along the remainder of the drive, easily visible now against the frosty parkland, though no lights were showing from the school. For the most part they were silent, but just once Eloise said, "At this time of night, and they were only attacking me," and then she became quiet again.

She showed him to a side door and Will worked open the lock. Once inside, she said, "We can go to my room – lucky that I'm in on my own this term."

"Can we be overheard there?"

She shook her head. "It's nicely tucked round a corner on its own. But we'll have to be quiet getting there."

The school was quite dark, but it said something for how well Eloise knew the place that she walked ahead of him with as much confidence as if every light was on. When they reached her room, she shut the door behind them, drew the curtains, placed a scarf over the bedside lamp and turned it on. She searched in a cupboard for something, then said, "I'll be back in a minute."

Will got the scent of blood as she walked out, almost as if the blood sought him out, calling like a siren to tempt him where he knew he could not go. He heard her walking along the corridor, could hear and sense beyond her the quiet, sleeping breaths of other healthy children.

Will tried to put it out of his mind by concentrating on the room in front of him. He stood exactly where she'd left him, letting his eyes slowly adapt to the dull light from the lamp, and took in the posters, one of a bare-chested young man with dark hair, another of a group of young men in dark clothes with make-up on their faces, another for a German production of Mozart's *The Magic Flute*.

There was a bed, a chair, a desk, various personal items, shelves full of books. He wanted to move across the room, to look at the books and see what she'd been reading, but he felt he didn't have permission somehow. This space was so intimate that, as well as he knew Eloise now, as deep as the bond was between them, it felt intrusive for him to be here.

He heard her return and when she came into the room, a strong smell of antiseptic masked the blood and she wore a plaster across the wound.

"It wasn't as bad as it looked – just a scratch really." She smiled as she closed the door again and said, "Come and make yourself comfortable."

Will stepped forward, forgetting to glance at the books as he pulled the chair from the desk and sat down. His eyes drifted from the bed in front of him and back up to the posters.

"Don't look at my posters – just too embarrassing."

Eloise pulled off her boots and sat cross-legged on the bed. She'd sat like this on the daybed in his chambers, which at least brought a touch of familiarity. His sitting here was no more a breach of intimacy than it had been for her to see where he lived.

"Are the people in those posters renowned in some way?"

She pointed behind her without looking, "He's an actor. They're a band – I used to think the one on the right was quite cute."

"But you don't any more?"

"No, because I have another cute boy now, just as unattainable as the ones in the posters." She laughed and he laughed a little too. "Actually, I only put them back up this term because the other girls would have been suspicious otherwise."

Will nodded, relaxing now as he said, "I like it in here; it has your scent, your presence. I feel peaceful in here."

Eloise smiled, but her mind was already elsewhere. "What happened out there?"

"Wyndham. It can only be. Otherwise what are we to believe, that it was some freakish natural occurrence? Wyndham brought it about, I'm sure of it, and in some way he must have discerned that you are important to my destiny, that it's easier to attack you, a normal, living girl, than it is to tackle me."

"Then he's a fool." Will looked confused and Eloise said, "If he's coming after me, he should have made his first attack during the day, when you're not around to protect me. Now I'll be on my guard whatever happens."

"It's a worthwhile point, but given the wound on your head, I don't think we should underestimate him. And I'm sure you didn't fail to notice that Chris was never away from us in the time between our confrontation and depositing us at the school gates."

Eloise thought back over the evening and said, "I hadn't thought about it, but you're right. Which means Chris . . ."

"No, it tells us nothing about Chris. It tells us only that Wyndham has some other source for our movements. And bear in mind, this is a man who summoned the ghost of my own brother to destroy me – his magical powers are probably such that he needn't rely on human assistance alone. So it seems we have to be more vigilant still." He looked at the clock next to her bed and said, "I should let you sleep. We can talk about Wyndham tomorrow night."

"OK. Oh, no, not tomorrow night, concert rehearsal." She pointed at an instrument case in the corner. "I play the violin – badly."

He stood and said, "The next night then, but be careful in the mean time." Eloise nodded and he reached out and brushed her cheek. She raised her own hand before he could take his away and pressed his fingers for a moment longer against the warmth of her face. Will smiled as she finally released him and he said, "Not quite as unattainable."

He left her and headed quickly out of the school, which was now in complete darkness. But he'd only walked a few paces when a crack of light appeared in one of the bedrooms high above. Will stopped and for a second the curtain was pulled back and a face appeared, looking out at the night before retreating again. And as much as Will had been intent on leaving, he remained now, staring up at the window. His interest was piqued because it was very late, and because the face which had briefly appeared was that of Marcus Jenkins.

6

The curtains hadn't closed completely when Marcus stepped back from the window, leaving enough of a gap for someone to see in from the outside – if that someone happened to be on the third floor.

Will moved closer, crouched and jumped up on to the stone window ledge of the room next to Marcus's. As little noise as he made, he didn't want to alert Marcus to his presence by leaping directly to his window. Now though he moved nimbly across the face of the wall and crouched on the ledge outside the lit room.

It took a moment or two for his vision to adjust, closing his eyes, opening them slowly. Marcus was sitting at the desk in his pyjamas, with a reading lamp angled so that it didn't shine across on the boy sleeping in the other bed.

He was writing in a book, showing great concentration, so much so that this time he didn't even seem to sense Will's presence outside. At first, Will wondered if Marcus was in some sort of trance, but the sleeping boy moved and Marcus turned to make sure

53

he hadn't woken before going back to his writing.

He appeared to fill the page he was on, then turned and wrote a little while longer before stopping. He looked deep in thought for a moment, then put down the pen and closed the book, which Will could now see was leather-bound. Carefully, Marcus put the book into the desk drawer, stood and turned off the lamp.

The room didn't descend into complete darkness, but took on a blue tinge. Only then did Will notice that the sleeping boy had a nightlight next to his bed. Marcus crossed the room and climbed into bed, turning immediately to face the wall.

Will waited for a few minutes, crouching on the narrow ledge, the wind lightly tugging at his hair and his coat. It wasn't a diary, he was certain of that, but what could be so important about that book that Marcus would wait until he could be assured of privacy before filling its pages?

The room looked lost in sleep now, the one boy sprawled on his back, Marcus completely still, as he had been since turning to face the wall. The window was shut firm and would be noisy to open, but Will was determined to find out what had been written in that book. He leapt away from the ledge, his coat billowing up behind him until he landed with a soft crunch on the frozen gravel below.

From there he made his way back into the school, climbing the main stairs and slipping quietly along the corridors, trying not to think about the sleeping world he was moving through. He counted along the doors on the section of the third floor that formed that outer wall – he'd reckoned on it being the fifth door along – and sure enough there was the blue tinge showing along the bottom of it.

He stood for a moment, listening through the heavy silence, then gently opened the door and stepped inside. Neither of the boys stirred, but still he waited, listening to the rhythm of their breaths, desperately trying not to think about the life in them and the scent of blood that seemed to fill the room.

They were asleep. Will stepped carefully over to the desk and slid open the drawer, removing the book that sat inside. Either Marcus trusted his room-mate entirely or his only concern was that the boy didn't see him writing in it.

Will took the book and leafed through the first few pages which were blank. He turned the pages quicker, then flicked through them, increasingly puzzled by the sea of white before him. None of it had been written on. It was definitely the same book and yet it was empty.

He traced his fingers across one of the pages, feeling for the indentations which might have been left by a pen, but there was nothing. He didn't understand it. He put the book back on the desk, open, and stared down at two dazzlingly blank white pages.

He had seen Marcus writing in it. He'd even seen him reach the end of a page and turn over, but there was nothing here – it could only be something of Wyndham's design. And it was clear now why Marcus might not want his friend to see him about his work.

Will heard a noise and glanced across at Marcus's bed, staring in confusion for a second at the crumpled shape of the duvet before realising Marcus was no longer beneath it. He turned quickly, surprised that he hadn't heard the boy getting up.

Marcus was standing behind him, quite calm, staring straight ahead as if through the top of Will's chest. Involuntarily, Will stepped backwards, pushing the drawer closed in the process – too much noise – but then stopped himself, the shock subsiding. And it subsided further with the realisation that Marcus was not awake. He stood quite still, his eyes staring ahead with an odd, cold patience, as if he was simply waiting for Will to move.

Will stepped to one side and Marcus approached the desk. Without looking down, he closed the book and placed it back in the drawer. Once the drawer was shut again, Marcus turned and crossed the room, climbing into bed and resuming the same position with his face to the wall.

Had he been sleepwalking or was even this some control of Wyndham's? And what was the sorcery of this book – some form of communication? Will wondered if Marcus had been using the book in some way to relay a general report or something more specific, the attack by the crows perhaps.

He looked at the boy sleeping peacefully, and though Will couldn't think why, he was desperate for Marcus to be no more than a spy. Will thought back to his behaviour that night by the river and it made him want to leave Marcus Jenkins unharmed, though he'd kill him without a second thought if he believed he was actively part of a scheme to hurt Eloise.

It was something Will would have to find out one way or another, but for now he retreated, moving silently back into the corridor, closing the door behind him. He moved quickly, back down the stairs and then to the side door. Only as he was about to open it did he hesitate, sensing something behind him.

He turned and looked along the corridor that led off through the ground floor of the school. He'd heard nothing, could see nothing, but for a moment, he'd sensed there was someone there. There was no one there now, but had someone seen him come in, had the same person waited for him to leave? Will took a few steps along the corridor, but there was still no movement, no scent.

Perhaps he was simply spooked by the strangeness of what he'd just witnessed in Marcus's room. On the other hand, his instincts told him somebody had been there, and that served as a reminder that Wyndham undoubtedly had more than one person working for him in the school.

Will gave up and left, and set off across the parkland to the new house, but his thoughts were full of this troublesome sorcerer. Who was he, why so determined to destroy Will, possessed of how much power, how much knowledge?

Wyndham could summon the dead, that much Will had seen, and yet strangely Will was more unnerved by the oddity of that empty notebook, perhaps because it suggested a magic that worked on many different levels. And that thought in turn gave rise to another question – how dangerous was Marcus to Eloise?

The potential answers to that question filled him with fear. Without thinking, he reached up and held the broken half-medallion that hung round his neck and was surprised to find it warm, almost as if it had been resting against her flesh, not his.

The metal's heat radiated through his hand, reminding him of Eloise and her room. Will didn't understand how it could be so, but it reassured him nevertheless because it suggested they had a sorcery of their own, and because right now he held within his hand the only piece of warmth in that vast icy landscape.

7

At the time of my mother's collapse she had no way of knowing what this creature was that had reappeared in her life after so long an absence. Nor at the time could I fully understand the role she foresaw for me. Clearly she felt she had been haunted by a demon, and sensed in its return that it wished harm to her soul. What is more, for some unimaginable reason she saw in me, her youngest child, the one person who could save her from it.

Only with hindsight can I see that William of Mercia had no designs on my mother's soul. Indeed, given that he resisted his ample opportunities to feed on her, I still wonder to this day what interest he did have. I suspect further that he chanced upon her that night in 1742 quite by accident.

But when a small child receives entreaties from his mother, asking him to act as her protector, to study hard that he might be equipped for the role, what is his response likely to be? I was an enthusiastic soldier in her army against evil long before I even realised that it was evil we were fighting, or that she was training me not to be a foot soldier, but a general.

My father encouraged me further, seeing the apparent happiness and strength that the scheme brought to Lady Bowcastle. It helped too that it was a whim which could be afforded, for unlike many a younger son, I would not be required to become a clergyman or follow a military career to earn my living.

My mother was an only child and both families were equally wealthy. Most of my maternal grandfather's fortune was settled on me, as was that of a childless maternal great-uncle. I would have no title, but my fortune would rival my brother's.

So it was decided. I would not go to boarding school. I would be kept close, all the better to offer my mother constant assurance of my progress, and carefully selected tutors would be brought to me. For though I studied many of the subjects familiar to my contemporaries, I studied them towards specific ends and saw them supplemented by lessons of a rather more exotic nature.

I learned Latin and Greek, better to appreciate the classics, but also that I might understand the arcane and mysterious texts that were acquired for me. I learned science that I might understand the riddles of the world and be better equipped for the work that lay ahead. I *enjoyed sporting pursuits, though with much more emphasis on the combat skills my mother imagined I would sooner or later require.*

I studied the occult too, with a stream of scholars and priests brought to me from all over these islands, and from France, Germany, Italy and beyond. I devoured this part of my curriculum, but knew from the outset that it was the one subject I was not to discuss freely outside of the schoolroom. Even my mother never discussed it with me, all the better to encourage my discretion.

Such was the liveliness of my intellect and the completeness of my general education that I hardly wanted for other subjects of polite conversation. Indeed, to the wider world, I was a bright but ordinary boy of my class, enjoying healthy outdoor pursuits and the society of my equals. And in that way, the eager child grew into an accomplished young man.

In the final year or so I spent with my family I was considered a figure of note – handsome enough, more than wealthy enough, blessed with various talents. With some retrospective irony, it was openly speculated upon, in that last summer, that I might prove an ideal match for Lady Maria Dangrave, eldest daughter of the Earl of Mercia.

She would have made a fine match too, pretty and

intelligent, with a wry humour, and I think we liked each other well enough. Of course, little could I have known then that she was of the same bloodstock as the demon that had unwittingly shaped me.

Lady Maria Dangrave. I think back on her now, her curls of fair hair, her lively eyes, delicate lips, and I cannot help but think what a short, happy life I might have lived with her. I say this even as I know it is pointless to think on it, for it wasn't to be.

Within twelve months of each other, my great-uncle and my grandfather had died, and my mother decided the time had come to conclude my education abroad. I have sometimes wondered if she was driven by the alarm she felt at my growing attachment to Maria. Whatever her motive, the timing was fortuitous in one regard – after all, it's the only reason I'm telling my story now, two hundred years after I should have died an old man.

8

When Will got to the house, he turned and walked across the east lawns instead of going inside. He reached the ruins and strolled among them. It was something he'd avoided until now because it filled him with sadness to see the remnants of these walls standing jagged like broken teeth.

So much of his world had survived in the city, and at times he would glance along streets or up at the walls or at the church itself and momentarily forget that he'd been cast adrift in the future. Yet Marland, the image of which was still so firmly fixed in his mind, the monks and their herb gardens and apiaries and their devotions, the quiet order and beauty of it all, had been reduced to these fallen walls.

He'd come now only because something had occurred to him, something that should have suggested itself earlier. Some of the walls had been so demolished as to leave something resembling a raised stone footpath in places, and he clambered about on it, and looked at the views into all those lost rooms. He tried not to think of what had once been there, but of another memory.

And as he climbed up on to a small buttress of stones and looked across to an ornate window arch that appeared almost free-standing, the images slipped into place and he knew this was it. This was the place he'd been dreaming of since November, the ruins among which he'd walked constantly with Eloise on a summer's day.

He stepped down on to the grass, which crunched beneath him, and he sat on the wall and looked across at the window arch and the other views across the ruins. He couldn't begin to think why he was being tormented with dreams of something he could never see. Yes, he could see these ruins in front of him now, he could bring Eloise here, but he could never recreate those visions.

That sunlit afternoon was something that could never and would never be his, just as his relationship with Eloise could never be what it often seemed to be in those dreams. It was a uniquely cruel torture that his mind should show him glimpses again and again of things he wasn't permitted to know.

He sat there for a while, his mind skipping back and forth between his memories of the dreams and the strange, conflicting thoughts brought on by being in Eloise's room. He wished he could see meaning in it, but there was none, only that she was a beautiful girl, that he wished she had lived and been of his class in 1256, that he had not fallen sick – too many wishes.

Will stood abruptly, a surge of energy coming on the back of all that frustration, and walked quickly back to the house. Wallowing in regret was all very well, but he had too much to do before dawn, and before he could bring Eloise here again. He had feared too much for her in those tunnels, and realised only now how foolish he had been to take her there unprepared. The attack by the crows had convinced him that he couldn't let his guard drop. It had shown him that, despite what Eloise might have thought, he wasn't always strong enough and couldn't always protect her.

Something down there had also put fear into him, though he couldn't think what he had to fear, except perhaps the truth of who he was. Whatever it was, he was determined he would face it alone before being so reckless as to expose Eloise to it again.

Will headed for the billiard room once he was inside the house. There was a display of three sabres on the wall above the table and he took one down, then another, testing their weight and feel. He selected one, put the other back in its place and headed for the library.

He'd have to replace the sabre before daybreak

because it seemed every day or so someone came and checked over the house and he wouldn't want its absence to be noted. He looked at the clock in the hall as he passed through it, estimating he had six hours, maybe only five, if he wanted to be sure of being back in the cellars before dawn.

The cellars – that was the worst of it, spending the daylight hours in those cellars with almost nothing to distract him from the gnawing need for blood. It was even worse when he could hear someone in the house above, and if the caretaker or security guard, whoever it was looking after the house, had ventured into the cellars at any point, Will wasn't sure he'd have been able to exercise the self-control that had kept him from notice all these centuries.

In the library he pressed the button to the side of the bookshelves that opened the secret panel, stepped inside and let the door close behind him. He slid the sabre through his belt and placed his hands on the wall. The mechanism ground into motion and the wall slid away to reveal the entrance to the steps.

Will stared, but didn't move. When he did move, it was first to reach for his dark glasses, then to pull the sabre free. The lights were on in the tunnels, but he remembered clearly that they'd turned them off on leaving.

It reminded him too readily of the last time they'd found lights on unexpectedly, in the cathedral library, and he wondered if once again it was a sign that one of Wyndham's apparently numerous disciples was also searching the tunnel complex.

He couldn't pick up a scent, nothing at all, and could hear nothing either, but the labyrinth was so vast it was possible he wouldn't be able to detect another visitor from here anyway. He reached out to the light switch, reasoning that he might as well turn his own superior night vision to his advantage if he was about to face an enemy. But he flicked the switch first one way, then the other, and the lights remained on.

Will laughed a little to himself, then louder, finally finding some admiration for this Wyndham, for his ingenuity and his determination, for his irritating ability to throw obstacles in Will's way. It was even more amusing for the fact that Will didn't even know where he was meant to be heading – Wyndham would have probably had just as much success in denying Will his destiny by simply leaving him alone, floundering in ignorance.

He took his glasses off and stared down into the lights, which were not as bright as those he regularly encountered in the city. The pain, which was still considerable, even helped take his mind off his hunger, and slowly he adjusted until his vision was unimpaired. It was a small gesture, perhaps even petty, but it was his way of throwing the gauntlet back at the sorcerer, making clear that he would need more than electrical trickery to defeat William of Mercia.

He closed the wall behind him and descended the steps, listening, inhaling deeply, ready to strike first at whomever or whatever he encountered.

At the bottom of the steps he followed the connecting tunnel to the beginning of the labyrinth proper, then turned left instead of right, aiming to cover all of the remaining tunnels in Eloise's absence. If there were hiding places or signs that others were also here, he wanted to find them.

The decoration was the same everywhere Will looked, the runic writing and other even more archaic scripts, the symbols, paintings of men and fantastic creatures. It had undoubtedly been a massive undertaking, and that made it seem all the more significant that the pentagonal chamber had walls that were almost bare.

Something else was the same throughout, that brooding sense of menace he'd experienced the first time. He walked in silence. The air carried only the smell of dust, but he was so certain he was heading towards something that he felt himself tensing with each corner or opening he approached.

Yet, as with the first visit, each turn revealed nothing, just the gloomy tunnel leading away to another corner, another junction. It didn't matter how many times he failed to be confronted by someone, didn't matter that he sensed nothing living, he still expected the next turn to bring him face to face with . . . he knew not what.

Finally Will reached the pentagonal chamber, coming to it from one of the other four lit entrances. There was the fifth tunnel too, still in darkness, and as Will moved about the chamber, he tried to keep it in his line of sight, never turning his back on it.

He looked at the bronze relief on the floor, the boar's head medallion and the four swords, each leading out to a point on the walls where those runic names had been inscribed. He crouched down and touched the boar's head, almost expecting it to be warm as the medallion had been warm around his neck – it wasn't, and now when he reached up, he realised there was no longer any warmth coming from his own fragment of bronze.

He stood again, looking at the walls. Had those ancient artists left this room bare to highlight the four names, the four swordsmen? A thought sprang into his mind and he immediately wished he hadn't left Jex's notebook in the city – could these four names, these four swords, represent the four kings Jex had spoken of in his book? And if so, was it possible that one of these inscriptions was an ancient form of the name Lorcan Labraid? He had read it in the notebook, he was sure – Lorcan Labraid was the Suspended King, one of the four. If Will was right, this chamber was the closest he had been to finding him.

He walked around the room, touching each of the names in turn, a token gesture, wanting to touch the name of the evil that had done this to him, wanting in some way to bring himself closer to the destiny that had been mapped out for him that night so long ago. And now that the thought had planted itself, he stared again at the relief in the floor, seeing a new meaning in it. The boar's head represented Will and his family, the Mercian Earls who had been so cruelly treated, held prisoner by the swords of these four barbarian kings.

He heard a noise, and looked up, immediately readying his sword. Had it been a footstep? He took in the air, picking up nothing, but he had heard a noise and it had come from the one place he had known he would have to face sooner or later, the darkened tunnel.

Will took a step towards it and then stopped again as the lights flickered on along its length and in the chamber that lay maybe twenty paces beyond. It was almost as if he was being invited in. The only thing he didn't know was the identity of the person or creature issuing the invitation.

He walked on, not hesitating this time, but heading directly into the tunnel. He was halfway along it when the lights flickered, for a second only, a rapid descent into darkness and an equally sudden return to light. And now Will felt the cold in his spine again because in that second a figure had walked past the far entrance.

The chamber ahead appeared empty now, but he had seen a figure cross, he was certain of it. He walked on, cautious, ready to strike first, and was almost at the end of the tunnel when once again the lights blacked out before firing back more brightly than before, or so it seemed.

Will's eyes smarted against the sudden glare, but he stood his ground, holding his sabre at arm's length in front of him. He blinked, desperate to get his vision back, because one thing he could see through the light blindness – he was no longer alone.

A figure stood in the middle of the chamber, facing him, fair-haired, wearing a dark suit and a dog collar, looking quite alive – Reverend Fairburn, Wyndham's spy from the cathedral library. He looked as solid as he had in the moments before falling to his death.

Will stepped into the circular chamber, his sword still at the ready, but Fairburn looked down at it and said, "There's no need for that, nor would it be of much use – I'm an apparition."

Will looked around the chamber. He noticed the walls here were decorated, unlike the chamber with the bronze relief, but all he really wanted to see was that they were alone in there. Once satisfied of that, Will slipped the sword back into his belt, but moved away from the tunnel and edged round the chamber until he could see both the spirit and the way out.

He looked at the ghost of Fairburn and said, "Is it not enough that Wyndham made you his servant in life? Now he enslaves you even in death, denying you your peace."

"Oh, I came gladly for this task. You seek your destiny, isn't that so?"

"We all seek our destinies in one way or another."

"True. Well, William of Mercia, prepare yourself because I'm about to show you yours."

Will laughed and said, "You're about to show me what Wyndham would have me believe. You may be a spirit, you may have been dragged from the next world just as my brother was, but neither you nor Wyndham know any more about my destiny than I do. Tell me Wyndham's lies if you wish, but they will be just that, lies."

Fairburn's expression didn't change. He turned and stared directly at Will, the thing he had tried to avoid so much at their last meeting, and said, "You killed me. I

73

know I jumped, but it was the lesser evil. You killed me, William of Mercia, that is why I am here. I am about to show you the true nature of your destiny, and trust me, you will know it to be the truth and you will despair."

9

"Do your worst," said Will, sceptical and yet still intrigued. "Whatever my destiny, I know my own heart."

"Do you?"

Will had stepped back against the wall to prepare for whatever was about to happen, his left hand still poised to reach for his sword if needed. Fairburn remained in the middle of the chamber, but raised his hands now as if invoking a short prayer. When he lowered them again, he smiled and said, "Behold."

For a moment nothing happened, but then Will noticed the walls had become less solid around them, shimmering in the way he remembered the air on the hottest summer days. Across the room, a figure appeared, at first like a carved stone relief within the wall, then taking more shape, then colour, before emerging solid and real into the chamber.

Another ghost, another he recognised, from the bare feet and grubby blue top, the scraggly beard. The spirit walked past Fairburn, heading towards a point just to the right of Will where he disappeared into the wall as if made of nothing more substantial than mist. He had looked solid for the time he'd been within the chamber and yet something had been missing. He hadn't looked at Will as Fairburn had, hadn't looked at anything, his eyes and expression vacant.

"You recognised him, of course," said Fairburn once the figure had disappeared. "He called himself Jex. His real name, if it concerns you, was Stephen Leonard. He was a troubled young man, but healthy, a perfect victim . . . for you."

Even as Fairburn spoke, another figure was emerging out of the walls, taking on form and colour before breaking free, and Will felt his certainties crumble at the sight of her. He had forgotten the precise likeness of her face, and saw now that despite the short hair, the slightly different clothes, she bore more than a passing resemblance to Eloise and could so easily have been her. With an additional twinge of regret, he remembered how playful her eyes had been, and saw now how dulled and empty they were, how lost her expression.

"Did you even know her name? Helen, and she was just fourteen years old back in 1988. A runaway, naturally, one of the many unlucky vulnerable people to have crossed your path."

Even as Fairburn spoke, two more figures were emerging from the walls, then a third. And when Will looked, Helen – whose name he hadn't known, it was true – had disappeared.

Fairburn started to speak, but Will interrupted, saying, "Why do they not see me as you do? These are not spirits, these are mere images, impressions of people who once existed."

Half a dozen were crossing the chamber in different directions in front of him. Two crossed paths, the apparitions passing through each other and becoming some misty amalgam before reforming again and continuing their journey towards the more total oblivion of the chamber wall.

Fairburn said, "I was your most recent victim, no less than any of these, but I was fortunate indeed to take my own life before you could perform your wickedness upon me. You see, William of Mercia, a spirit and a soul are two different things, and you took their souls when you killed them. This is what you made of them, empty vessels wandering the afterlife with no purpose, no reward. You didn't just rob them of life, you robbed them of so much more."

Will shook his head, struggling to accept these words, struggling with the scores of spirits now criss-crossing the room in front of him, some disappearing into the walls either side of him, so close that he could have reached out and touched them.

The air seemed to be crackling now, charged with all this energy as more and more spirits emerged. And Fairburn was becoming triumphant and manic, calling out comments here and there as each new spirit appeared.

"This woman was with child when you killed her, two deaths, not one. Ah, George Cuthbertson, 1813, but he was merely a stable boy, nothing to a nobleman like you, hardly worthy of consideration. And here we are in 1741, young Tom, fresh to the city – how generous the poor have been to you, William of Mercia."

One thing Will could not deny was that these were all his victims, and the face of every one of them found a match in his memory, even after all this time. He had often thought of them, cushioned only by the knowledge of the many more deaths he had seen during his long existence.

But if what the spirit of Fairburn said was true, there was no context that would excuse his actions. He had condemned these people not to death but to an eternal limbo, stripped of the very essence of who they had been.

Across the crowded chamber, a young girl emerged from the wall and Will could not stop himself calling out, "Kate!" But she did not hear or see him, and to stare at her vacant expression was too painful a reminder of how she had once laughed and made him laugh, and how she had so willingly volunteered to be bitten in the hope of becoming his companion.

"Good Kate," cried Fairburn. "It would have been far, far better for her had the plague taken her, and not your tainted act of friendship."

"Are their souls gone forever?"

Fairburn ignored him at first, and appeared almost to be carrying out a headcount of the dozens of spirits emerging and disappearing all across the chamber. Finally, it seemed, the numbers were declining again.

"Nothing is forever, even you. Perhaps especially you. When you die, their souls will be released from you and restored to them. I don't know what will happen to yours, but if there's any justice, it will be destroyed."

"I care nothing for what happens to my soul. But nor do I believe you. It is possible, I will allow, that I have reduced them to this, but I would know if I carried all these souls within me."

Again Fairburn appeared not to be listening. There were only four spirits left in the chamber, and as each disappeared into the walls, he looked more and more puzzled.

Only Will and Fairburn were now left in the room, but Fairburn looked up into the air, lost in calculation as he said, "Eight hundred and forty-three, I make forty-four, but there should be one more . . ." With an air of cheap theatricality, he fixed his gaze on Will and said, "How could I have forgotten?"

He waved his hand at the far wall with a flourish and it immediately showed the outline of a human form. It took shape: a woman, wearing a rich blue dress of the kind worn in Will's childhood, golden hair, pale skin. She stepped out on to the floor of the chamber, a young woman of radiant beauty, at once both familiar and unknown to him.

She wasn't like the others, and she stared about the chamber as if confused, wondering how she came to be here. These spirits had all been summoned by Wyndham, but this one alone appeared to know that it had not wished to be brought forth.

Coaxing, Fairburn said, "Come, spirit, come into the chamber." She was walking towards the centre of the room, but not apparently in response to Fairburn's instructions.

The spirit looked past Fairburn and saw Will for the first time, and now she stopped and stared, and a slight hopeful smile formed on her lips. It faded as she glanced at Fairburn and when she turned her attention back to Will, she seemed eager to impart some message to him.

She did not speak, but reached up and took hold of

a pendant hanging round her neck, brandishing it at Will as she stared at him, smiling again, with something that looked like encouragement. Then she let go and put her finger to her lips. Only as she turned away did the smile fade, a deep and private sadness taking hold of her features.

"Stay a while, spirit," said Fairburn. But the lady walked a circle round the vicar, and gradually sank into the floor as she did so, as if descending a wide spiral staircase. "Spirit, this distresses you, I know, but you are commanded to stay! See here the evil before us . . ." But the spirit had gone.

Will didn't know what to think. Had this been a victim, she would hardly have smiled, or made intimate gestures that had certainly been meant to communicate something, even if the meaning had been lost on him. Besides, he would have remembered a victim so striking from so early on in the course of his sickness.

Fairburn had looked briefly deflated, but he rallied and looked at Will, shaking his head. "It's hardly a surprise that your first victim should find it so disturbing to see what you've become."

"My first victim? I think not – I have never seen that fair lady before."

"Your mother, William of Mercia, you have just seen the spirit of your mother."

Will knew instantly that it was true, though he had never seen her, and he felt as if he'd received a body blow. If he'd had tears, he would have shed them all gladly now for the mother he had never known.

"My mother died in childbirth."

"Your mother was murdered during childbirth, by those who served you even then, to protect your poisoned legacy."

"You lie," said Will, though he was aware of his own voice sounding weak, his thoughts struggling to hold fast against this onslaught.

"Lie? Did I not show you your destiny? Aside from me and the woman whose grave misfortune it was to give birth to you, you can hardly deny the eight hundred and forty-three souls you have taken – that wicked tally is your destiny, and merely the first act of all that is to come."

Will had been alive long enough to know that there was no lie greater than that which was held up by facts. These were facts, all these many victims, but he still believed, had to believe, that there was a lie at the bottom of all this, a lie created by Wyndham in his battle to destroy him.

"I don't accept that – it is the sickness I have been cursed with, and it has been a curse, but my destiny is to escape it. As I have said before, I know my own heart."

Fairburn looked full of hatred as he said, "Your heart, as I believe you know, stopped beating a very long time ago. Accept death, William of Mercia, and release the souls of these good people. That is Mr Wyndham's offer – accept death willingly, gratefully, or he will destroy you, and the torment he will inflict will be greater than hell itself could offer."

"If *Mr* Wyndham is so powerful, why does he not tell me these things himself?"

"He will, when the time is right."

"Of course, when the time is right." Suddenly Will remembered Asmund's comment about the many obstacles faced in the life of a great man, then his suggestion that Will had been no random victim, that his sickness had been long planned. "You spoke of my poisoned legacy – what did you mean by it? Or was that just another piece of embroidery to make me believe my mother was murdered on my behalf?"

Fairburn looked uncertain how to respond for a moment, then closed his eyes and whispered, "Do I tell him that much at least?"

So not only had he been summoned by Wyndham, he was in communion with him even now, just as Asmund had been with his master. If Lorcan Labraid had only communicated with Will in much the same way, this entire process would have been a great deal simpler.

Fairburn nodded, having been given approval, and said, "William of Mercia, this is your vile truth – the bloodlines of the four vampire kings meet within your person and yours alone, making you the one of whom these evil prophecies speak." He gestured to the inscriptions on the walls around them. "That is why your mother was murdered, to ensure there would not be another to challenge your uniquely wicked claim."

As he spoke, Fairburn began to look less solid, a thin mist emanating from him, reducing him to transparency, to vapour.

"What about my destiny? What do you know of it?"

At first it seemed there would be no reply, but at the last, Fairburn's voice emerged from the final swirling fragments of his form.

"It is not in front of you."

Fairburn had gone and Will was alone in the chamber. He tried to think what Fairburn might have meant by those words, trying to imagine how his destiny might be behind him rather than ahead of him. It took Will a minute or two to see a different meaning, one that was not a riddle but literal.

He turned and looked with horror at the painting in front of which he'd been standing all this time. There, among countless inscriptions, was a picture of a king sitting on a throne, and though the art was primitive, it was undoubtedly intended to be Will's likeness.

Surrounding him, just as they surrounded the boar's head relief in the neighbouring chamber, forming a cross, were the four swords. Most disturbingly, the throne sat on top of a small hill, but on closer inspection, the mount revealed itself to be made of naked and mutilated bodies, blood-spattered, faces wracked with anguish and pain.

Will recoiled from it, but he was angry too. He had already been dragged down into wickedness by this sickness, but he would be dragged no further. He refused to accept that this image represented anything of his future and he strode out of the chamber – he had done evil things, but he was not evil, and evil would not, could not be his destiny.

It left him more determined than ever to press ahead. As troubled as he was by seeing his victims, as shocked by the possible truth of destroying their souls, he had to keep going or everything, including those eight hundred and forty-three deaths, would have been pointless.

With nothing more that he could do for the time being, Will simply walked, fast, exploring passage after passage until each one and the overall pattern of the labyrinth were familiar to him. There was no other feature in there and all paths led back eventually to the pentagonal chamber.

He reached it again and again, but even though he had been in the circular chamber once, he could not bring himself to walk the once-dark corridor to look at it a second time. The memories already associated with that second chamber, of the wall painting, of the soulless faces of his victims, of his mother, were still too troubling.

Yet as he stood for the last time next to the bronze relief, staring at the tunnel which had taken him there, the thought of his mother offered some reassurance. She had recognised him, had she not, suggesting her spirit had watched over him as he'd grown. And she had tried to impart some advice, even encouragement, something she surely would not have done if only evil awaited him.

Will thought of her clutching the pendant round her neck, but he had not seen the item of jewellery and could not now know what it had signified. Unless . . . He reached up and held the broken medallion round his own neck, wondering if this was what she'd been trying to tell him, to think on this medallion and all it promised. It was cold in his hand now, but it had been warm, and somewhere else its twin was warm against Eloise's skin. It promised a different future to the one painted by Fairburn, and that different future was the only one Will dared imagine.

10

Will returned to the house, put the sabre back where it belonged and descended into the cellars. It was another hour before he felt that slight telltale prickling on his skin, warning him that the sun had struggled above the eastern horizon.

Now his imprisonment here was total, for the next eight hours or so anyway. He paced from cellar to cellar, trying and failing to take his mind off the needling hunger for blood that swept over him, carrying him along. It was a craving made even more unbearable by the recently rekindled memories of his many past victims.

Helen, whose name he had not known, had been taken in the late autumn of 1988, around the same time of year that he'd met Eloise. And her sacrifice had been made for what now seemed the most meagre of reasons, sustaining him only through the winter months and into the spring when he'd hibernated again.

Then he'd slept for twenty years, during which time a boy called Stephen Leonard had grown into a man, unknowingly preparing himself for the role of Will's next victim. Nor did it ease Will's mind to know that the boy, Jex as he'd become, had been chosen by other forces before Will had found him.

It was painful to think back on it, and worse to know that there would be an eight hundred and forty-fourth victim, that there had to be because Will's own spirit seemed to be gnawing away at him, crying out for the sustenance it needed.

At some point during the morning hours, he heard someone in the house above, a man, whistling as he went about his business. Will's hunger for blood intensified and it was a relief to hear the slamming of an outer door, the removal of a temptation he could only have resisted for so long.

It felt at times as if these daylight hours would never end, and he left the cellars and the house almost as soon as darkness had fallen. The moon was already above the horizon, approaching its full state and creating a small amount of discomfort on Will's skin, but he didn't care, such was the liberation of being out on the frozen landscape after being trapped since the beginning of the day.

He walked about the woods for a couple of hours and once night had firmly established itself, he strolled towards the school. He knew that Eloise was busy this evening, but he had to go, if only to see her from afar, to be near her.

Even as he came close to the school, he could hear music, but the hall it came from wasn't visible from the outside. He returned to his usual spot, looking into the Dangrave House common room from a safe distance.

It was half empty tonight, but there was Marcus Jenkins, sitting at a table playing chess with his friend. Marcus picked up the black queen, hesitated for a moment and then used it to take one of his opponent's pieces. His friend said something, shaking his head in irritation, but also acknowledging the skill of the move.

Marcus answered, smiling, but then turned and looked directly at Will, returning to the pattern that had been broken only the previous night outside his bedroom. It was unnerving, his eyes appearing to reach out beyond the window, and even if Marcus could only see his own reflection, Will wondered what it was exactly that he saw there.

Marcus turned away again, but it left Will uneasy, thinking back on the empty book, the sleepwalker's stare. Marcus was Wyndham's spy, but it was more than that, some mysterious quality that lay within the boy, something Will had sensed even the first time they'd met.

Will watched for a few moments more before heading

off into the woods that bordered the drive, exploring them for anything that might explain the attack of the previous evening. He could hear crows roosting in the branches high above him now, but they seemed to pay no attention to him, just as they had failed to notice him the night before.

By the time he headed back to the school, the night was drawing on. He came within a hundred paces of a female teacher standing by one of the doors, huddled against the cold as she whispered into a phone, talking to a boyfriend. Will caught the scent of her on the crisp air and veered to the right to escape the ever-present temptation – she was young, and healthy.

The common room was empty now and as he stood there, a male teacher came in, did a quick check of the room and turned off the light before leaving again. There were some lights on upstairs, though not Marcus's, and the evening was drawing to a close for Marland Abbey School, just as it was beginning for Will.

He remained for a minute longer, as if the common room was still full of people, but then got the uncomfortable sense once more that someone was watching him. He looked up – the same darkened window on the top floor – making a mental note of which room it was.

He took a few more backward steps, and a little

while later, as more lights died in the windows and sleep descended, he accepted he wouldn't see Eloise tonight. It was for the best – he worried that he was depriving her of sleep as it was. Reluctantly he turned and strolled back towards the new house, heading for the stand of trees that obscured each from the other.

And he'd almost reached the trees before he realised he was not walking alone. Silently and without ceremony, robed figures had appeared a little way to the left and right of him – two of the witches Eloise had asked about only the night before.

Will stopped and turned. Four more of the witches followed behind, but stopped now at a slight distance, their heads bowed, obscuring the absent faces.

"What do you want of me?"

At first there was no response, and when it did come, it was from behind him. "To do your duty, nothing more."

He turned to see the seventh standing facing him, close to the trees he'd been approaching just a moment before. She alone showed her face, almost featureless, only darker shadows where her eyes and mouth had once been.

"My duty?"

"To protect." The other six spirits had started walking towards her and left him behind now on the frosted park. "You need the girl, and the sorcerer knows it, which is why the girl needs you." Will was about to speak when she raised her arm, pointing past him to the school, urgent as she said, "Now, William of Mercia, she needs you now!"

He felt a sudden surge of fear for Eloise and glanced over his shoulder at the school, an ominously dark outline against the moonlight.

"She's in danger right now?"

But when he turned back again, the spirits had gone.

He ran at full speed across the parkland, his nerves torn, fearing what he might be running towards. The spirits hadn't intervened the previous night, an attack that had been serious enough in itself, so what was happening to Eloise now that they had felt the need to come to him?

He entered through the side door Eloise had showed him, leaping up the stairs and along the corridors with little concern for being spotted or disturbing anyone. He reached Eloise's door, opened it, turned on the light so as not to alarm her and closed the door again as his eyes smarted.

Even when he could see, he struggled to believe what he was looking at. Eloise lay on her back, asleep, wearing a long red cotton nightshirt – but she was not on her bed, she was floating above it and moving slowly as if drawn by a magnetic power. The window had been thrown wide open and Eloise was drifting towards it.

This wasn't just an attempt to harm Eloise, but to kill her. If this was Wyndham's determination, to kill Eloise, it meant that Will needed her alive to fulfil his destiny, whatever that destiny proved to be. He would not let Wyndham win, but he knew something else too, knew it in every fibre of his being – he would kill himself before he allowed any harm to come to Eloise.

This time at least he could keep her safe. He closed the window first, pulling hard, as if against another hand that was struggling to keep it open. He locked it and drew the curtains lest her light be seen from outside. Eloise seemed to stop moving as soon as the window was closed, but still she hovered shoulder-height above the bed.

Will moved his hands around her, trying to find signs of whichever force held her like that. There was nothing he could detect. He said her name quietly, moving his mouth close to her ear and saying it again, but she would not wake.

He needed to get her back on to the bed, so he placed one hand on top of her stomach, the other across her thighs and gently pressed down, once again fighting against some unseen force, but gradually winning. And all the while he was tormented, by her warmth, by the softness of her flesh through the thin material of the nightshirt. Nor was this a longing for blood, that hunger almost disappearing when he was with her, but a longing for that other life he dreamt of.

Finally she touched the bed and the force that had held her up seemed to subside, her weight easing into the mattress. At the same time, she opened her eyes, waking. She looked up, taking a moment to register his presence, then she smiled, puzzled and bemused.

"Will? What are you doing?"

"Forgive me," he said, taking his hands from her body. "This is not what it seems."

She laughed and said, "Sadly, I know that to be true, but . . . how weird. I've just realised I was dreaming about you. Sorry, forget that, what are you doing here?"

"The witches came to me. They told me that Wyndham knows I need you – that's why he's attacking you."

Eloise sat up in the bed. "So it *was* him last night? And by the way, it's been the talk of the school today – sixteen dead crows found on the drive. But . . ." She smiled again, saying, "But just now . . .?"

"The window was open and you were floating towards it."

"Floating? You mean, like levitating?"

"Yes."

She shuddered, and said, "I don't believe it – that's

what I was dreaming. I dreamt you were calling from outside and I flew down to you." She looked at the window as if finally taking in that his presence here was serious, that she had come close to being thrown to her death.

"Wyndham's trying to kill me?" Her voice was small, laced with a fear that concerned Will because she had been so brave, so fearless until now, and he realised that he needed her bravery, even relied on it in some way.

"I won't let that happen." He looked around the room and took a small wind chime that she had pinned to a cork noticeboard. He tied it round the window handle and said, "Make sure you hang this here each evening. That way, if the window is opened, you'll hear the chimes and wake."

Eloise nodded as he walked back to her, but then he stopped, spotting a diagram of chalk markings on the wooden floor under the bed. She jumped from the bed and looked at it herself.

"Someone's been in my room!" It seemed to outrage her more than the recent attempt on her life. She took a tissue and used it to rub away the chalk markings.

Once they'd gone, Will said, "Good, from now on you must check for marks like this, or for anything else in your room that seems out of place. You must consider yourself under attack at all times."

"But I don't get it. Why does he think killing me will stop you?"

"It seems Wyndham knows what we've only imagined till now, that my destiny can't be achieved without you. It's the only explanation."

Eloise smiled playfully and said, "You'd better keep me alive then."

She was teasing him, perhaps as a way of countering her own fear, but he said, "I would happily give up my destiny and this poor excuse for a life before I would see any harm come to you."

"Don't say that," she said, touching him lightly on the arm. "I need you as well, remember. That's what Jex said. So don't ever say that." She sat back on the bed and gestured for him to sit too.

As he sat down, he said, "I meant only to say that protecting you means everything to me."

"I know that." She smiled a little, but then said, "Isn't it funny, there I was complaining about a lack of incident, and now I've been attacked by crows, nearly thrown out of a window, and you've seen the spirits again."

Eloise seemed upbeat at these developments, but Will felt the need to bring her back down to earth, to make clear that with greater activity came greater danger.

"I saw more spirits last night."

"What do you mean? Your brother again?"

"No, Edward will trouble me no more. This was the very late Reverend Fairburn, doing Wyndham's bidding in death as he did in life. And Fairburn in turn introduced me to the ghosts of all my victims, and was even kind enough to count them – eight hundred and forty-three." Will decided against mentioning their soulless eyes or the explanation he'd been given for it, not least because he still wanted to believe it wasn't so. "Then there was the ghost of my mother, murdered when I was born, or so Fairburn told me."

"You saw your mother?" She looked moved by the revelation and Will remembered that Eloise had been orphaned in infancy, that she also carried that longing and curiosity to know the woman who'd given birth to her. He nodded and she said, "But why? I mean, why would they murder her when you were born?"

"To ensure that I alone carry the bloodline of the four vampire kings. It relates to the wording of some ancient prophecy or other." Again he stopped short of telling her about the painting on the chamber wall. Instead he said, "Of course, this was all related to me by Fairburn, speaking for Wyndham, so we don't know how true it is."

"It makes sense though. From four will come one – didn't it say that in Jex's notebook?"

"It signifies nothing."

She shook her head, dismissing his comment. "No, Will, it does, whether we want it to or not."

He heard a floorboard creak above, just someone shifting about in bed, but that in turn reminded him of the unseen watcher from the window.

"What's on the top floor of the school?"

"Some of the teachers live up there, a few storerooms, I think. Why?"

He stood up. "I'll be back shortly. I just want to check something."

"Maybe I could –" He put his hand up to stop her, but smiled reassurance and she settled back against the pillows.

He moved swiftly, along the corridor, up two flights of stairs, then along a narrower staircase on to the top-floor landing. A couple of the rooms showed lights under the doors, though they hadn't been visible from outside. He counted along, reaching what he thought was the room in question.

It was a storeroom. Will moved to the window and looked down, confident that this was where his watcher had been. But he had no way of knowing who had been up here, only that it hadn't been Marcus Jenkins and that Wyndham had more than one spy in the school.

He was about to leave, but spotted a box of chalk, which looked as if it had been placed hurriedly on a shelf just inside the door. Will supposed a school was full of chalk, but he still wondered if the same person who'd spied from here had also drawn the diagram under Eloise's bed.

He left, only hesitating near one of the lit rooms where he could hear a subdued conversation. It was two female teachers, one of them the young woman he'd seen talking on the phone earlier, whispering, laughing quietly, talking in gossipy tones about different teachers.

He listened in for a moment, hoping to hear something telling, but he found himself weakening again rapidly, the hunger pulling him into the void. He walked on, eager to get back to Eloise. The rest of the school was full of the swollen silence of sleep, all those young pulses, gently pumping the blood he so desperately needed.

It was a relief to get back into Eloise's room where he noticed immediately that she was dressed. Before he could say anything though, she jumped from the bed and took hold of him by the arms, obviously worried. "Oh my God, Will, what's up with you?"

"Nothing, I'm fine." She pulled him across the room and they sat on the bed together.

"You look . . . it's the blood, isn't it? It's horrible, I can't stand seeing you like this." She stroked his face, his hair, held his hands, as if trying to soothe the life back into him, tears beginning to form in her eyes. And ironically, her touch, her very presence, while not giving him what he needed, at least made the hunger ebb away again.

He smiled, trying to reassure her. "It looks worse than it feels. Trust me, I'm fine, and always better when I'm with you."

She fixed her eyes on him, searching for any hint that he was lying, then said, "Can I give you a hug, just for a second? Would that make it worse? Of course it would – what a ridiculous thing to say."

He shook his head and held her, the warmth of her body almost seeming to pass through him, and she nestled her head into his shoulder, exposing her warm, pale neck. As much as she soothed him normally, it was agonising to be so close to the richness of her blood, knowing how long it would sustain him, but he would not pull away, not until she was ready and comforted and reassured.

Eloise, almost as if she'd heard his thoughts, slowly eased away and sat back against the headboard of the bed. She nodded, looking a little embarrassed, acknowledging that intimacy was a trial for him, not a comfort.

He looked at her. "Why are you dressed?"

She smiled. "When I was cleaning away the chalk

marks, it triggered something and when you went off just now, it came to me. Did you find anything by the way?"

"Nothing important."

"OK. I remembered where I'd seen that bronze relief we found – the circle with the four swords around it. It might even be a boar's head, but it's not really visible any more." Will gave her a questioning look. "Henry's Maze. It's here in Henry's Maze, in a pentagonal clearing. So, OK, this might be a leap, but don't you think it's possible that the maze is a map . . ."

"Of the labyrinth." Will laughed a little, remembering his one meeting with old Henry, long ago in the cathedral library, seeing now that he of all people, his brother's distant descendant, might have been able to tell Will more than he'd ever realised. More than that, he thought back to the way Henry had looked at him, as if at a familiar ghost, and wondered if he'd recognised the likeness from the painting in the circular chamber. "So you want to explore the maze?"

"That's why I'm dressed," said Eloise. "Who knows what clues clever old Henry left for us. And if Wyndham's trying to kill me, all the more reason to get a move on."

Will nodded and stood. He'd explored the labyrinth and had found nothing new, but perhaps Henry, across his long life, *had* discovered its secrets, and had left clues to them in the maze as Eloise suggested.

But as they descended through the school in darkness, Will's mind also raced back up to the top floor, to that storeroom, focusing on the box of chalk. It simply served to remind him that they were struggling to find out, clue by clue, things that Wyndham already knew.

11

*T*o be a young man of means in that period was a wonderful thing. It was the Age of Enlightenment, of scientific and artistic exploration, the era of the Grand Tour. Yes, there were troubling little wars, minor inconveniences, petty crimes and illnesses to endure, but Europe in the middle of the eighteenth century was something to behold.

I left home with barely a backward glance, so fixed was I on the adventures ahead. I took only a valet, coachmen and a cook. The custom was to take a guide too – a bear-leader – but I took none, for my own knowledge had already surpassed that of anyone who might have accompanied me.

And in that manner I crossed the Channel and proceeded along the well-worn routes through France and Italy to the wonders of antiquity, meeting the same fellow travellers again and again, in Paris, then in Florence, in Rome.

My tour differed in some respects, naturally. For

one thing there was no time limit on my travels, no restrictions placed on the locations I might visit. More importantly, I was a young man on a mission and my itinerary took me to places unknown to the average grand tourist of the day. Even when I visited common stopping points – the University of Heidelberg, for example – I was there to study secret texts or to meet with obscure academics.

Oh, I saw such things on my travels, and have such memories. I've lived the better part of three centuries, yet I remember those journeys as if they were yesterday – the royal burial mounds of Gamla Uppsala in the twilight, the Catacombs of San Gennaro in Naples, seeing the lost castle of Graubünden emerging out of the morning mist. The memories are so real, it's as if I could reach out across the centuries and step back into them.

For more than a decade I followed this existence, not only as a scholar, but as a young man in love with life and all the pleasures it had to offer. Despite all my preparations for battle, I never encountered a demon, nor even talk of demons that was worth listening to. It was the summer of a mayfly, or so I thought.

It was in the last gasp of my youth that I briefly tired of Europe and visited the Near East, journeying to the Pyramids at Giza, then on to the site of Memphis. The location of the ancient capital was known, but today's history books would have it that it was not excavated until Napoleon's army arrived some half a century later. In this, at least, the history books are wrong.

When I arrived, I found there, at what I now know to be the Necropolis, the camp of a most extraordinary man who called himself only Rossinière. Teams of native bearers were working on his behalf, digging among the ruins, yet though they found many artefacts, he showed little interest and was happy for the natives to spirit them away. He was looking for only one artefact in that ancient burial site and he never told me what it was or if he found it.

I have no complaint – I learned almost all that I know from that man. He was of noble birth, I knew that much, but I knew neither his nationality, nor his real name, for I'm certain it was not Rossinière. All that really matters is that he took me under his wing.

As we sat by the fire one night, discussing the stars suspended so closely above our heads, he looked lost in meditation briefly and said, "Might I tell you something, Wyndham?" I became uneasy, but I looked at his handsome and youthful face glowing in the light of the flames and relaxed again. As if to put me further at ease, he looked in my direction and smiled as he said, "It's my birthday today."

I congratulated him and asked him how old he was. I assumed he was a year or two older than me, but sensed he had learned rather more in his time and weathered a little better.

Rossinière looked away again, his eyes lost in the dancing flames as he said, "That's really what I wanted to tell you. I'm one hundred and forty-two years old." I didn't respond, but he read my initial thoughts, saying, "Don't worry, I have not been too long in the sun, I have no fever, and you are quite right not to believe me. I could try to prove it to you in many ways, but I can think of only one that is indisputable."

Something about the way he spoke assured me that he was telling the truth, that this man who sat before me had been born in 1624. My next thought was for the proximity of my weapons because I wondered if I had at last encountered such a demon as had haunted my mother.

"What are you?"

He smiled again. "Just a man, Wyndham, just a man like you, curious like you, desirous of more time like you. I am the way I am because of my own efforts, not through witchcraft or devilry."

Was I to believe him? In the previous ten years or so I had met plenty of fakers and cheats who would have travellers believe any number of tall tales.

"You said there was one way of proving your age beyond doubt."

"Not of proving my age, but of proving the possibility of it." He smiled again, but it was a lost smile, that of someone who might easily have lived for over a century. "I did have a fever, the week before you arrived here, and it might easily have killed me. Only then did I realise that nothing of what I know is written down – there's too much to write anyway – and that if I were to die, my secrets would die with me. Then you walked into my camp and I knew immediately you were a kindred spirit." He moved closer, staring into my eyes, and though he was now partly in shadow, his eyes seemed to fix me as if they were illuminated from within. "I'll teach you my secrets, Wyndham, how to have mastery over this world and the next, how to manipulate time so that you might pass through it without ageing a day. You know so much already, it would not be difficult to teach you the rest, if you want to learn."

What answer was I likely to give? I was thirty-two, and in the normal way of things I might have been thinking of returning home, establishing myself, settling into family life and a contented middle age. Rossinière turned past and future on their heads, and as I learned what he had to teach, I began to feel that thirty-two was just the very beginning of my life.

As to what he taught me, well at the time they might have been judged a sorcerer's arts, not least amongst them that secret of holding back the progress of time. To some even now this may seem to be magic; to scientists it might arouse the suspicion of fakery. To me though, both then and now, it is science, but a science that understands the full and mysterious complexity of the world in which we live.

We were not supernatural beings, Rossinière and I, but rather, as he had said, just men who were curious and who wanted more time. And as if I needed a reminder that our "sorcery" was not all-powerful, I received it when we returned to Cairo a month or so later.

I was met there by a letter which informed me of the death of my father. My mother, who despite her early breakdown was to outlive him by many years, sent word that I shouldn't return home, that my studies were more important.

It was easy to obey, of course, because my father would have been in the family crypt long before the news of his death had found me. But I'm ashamed to say that at that moment my mother's fixation on the demon which had haunted her seemed a childish pursuit, an act of ridiculous selfishness on her part.

Thanks to Rossinière, I was already making amazing breakthroughs in my mastery over the natural world, *and yet I still had so much to learn from him. I wept for my father whom I had not seen for over a decade, and despaired at my mother's foolish whims, but I was engaged in something so much greater than the concerns of their little and limited lives.*

I didn't share these thoughts with Rossinière – if I had, he might well have disagreed with me. He knew then what I had still to learn, that we would always be scholars, that the unknown would always be greater than the known. As it was, I dismissed the grieving Lady Bowcastle as a foolish woman who had never grown up, and another twenty-five years would pass before I truly understood the terrifying wisdom she'd possessed.

12

As they walked away from the school, Will said, "Won't you need a torch?"

Eloise shook her head. "I can't believe how light it is tonight anyway, but the paths in the maze are all lit with these cute little solar lamps."

"Solar? Like the sun?"

She smiled. "I'm sure they were around in the 1980s, at least, I think they were. They absorb the sunlight all day and then light up at night, not so bright that you'll need your sunglasses, but bright enough that I'll be able to see where I'm going."

"Good," he said, and looked up at the dazzling sphere of the moon, not wanting to tell her that he felt like putting on his sunglasses even now.

The entrance to the maze, it soon became apparent, corresponded to the point where the tunnel from the new house met the labyrinth. And as Henry had planted this maze centuries before the new house had been built, it suggested Thomas Heston-Dangrave had used a pre-existing entrance in his plans.

There was nothing here to suggest the grotesques and inscriptions that covered the labyrinth's tunnels, just walls of yew. Will and Eloise walked the paths quickly, their footsteps illuminated by the low-level lamps she'd told him about.

They reached the small pentagonal courtyard in the middle, and there, as Eloise had suggested, was the bronze relief planted into the gravel floor. The four swords were almost identical, but if there had ever been a boar's head on the round disc, it had been long worn smooth.

A small bench had been added to one side where it would provide shelter from the afternoon sun, but nothing else was visible here. Will pointed at one of the narrow avenues leading off the pentagon, the memory of that previously darkened tunnel causing a slight shiver to run through him.

"If the map is accurate, that should lead to a round clearing."

Eloise nodded and headed towards it, but with the previous evening still fresh in his mind, Will said, "Let me go first, just in case."

It was a maze though, nothing more, and after a few steps, they emerged into the circular clearing he'd expected to find there.

"This is where I saw the ghosts last night, in the chamber that matched this one."

"Beyond the darkened tunnel?" He nodded. Eloise pointed to the middle and said, "There's a bronze relief in here too."

Will wondered how she'd seen it when he hadn't noticed it himself, but then realised she was talking from memory, having long grown familiar with this maze. He followed her to the centre of the circle and looked down.

Eloise said, "It's a portcullis, but then I guess you know that. Is it the same as the one in the labyrinth?"

"In the labyrinth, this chamber has no bronze relief." Will looked around the circular clearing, seeing another bench, but nothing else, and thankfully nothing that hinted at the painting which represented him. "But Henry must have placed this here very deliberately. It must signify something."

Eloise crouched down, tracing her fingers across the relief as a blind person might do, and said, "A portcullis is a gateway. Whether you saw it or not, maybe there's some kind of gateway in that room."

It would make sense of his foreboding, of the fact that he had explored all the tunnels and found nothing else to bring him closer to Lorcan Labraid. And Will couldn't help but remember the way his mother's spirit, rather than passing through the walls as the others had done, had descended into the centre of the chamber as if by way of a spiral stairway. Had that been part of what she'd been trying to tell him, and if so, as guidance or warning?

"It can be the only meaning."

"Well, you don't sound particularly enthusiastic – I'd call this a breakthrough, wouldn't you?"

"Not all breakthroughs are equally welcome." Eloise looked confused and he said, "Think on this – a portcullis isn't merely a gateway, it's also a defence. If we find this gateway, if I can open it, we have no idea what we might unleash in the opening of it."

She stared at him for a second, apparently in disbelief. Finally she counted on her fingers as she said, "Your dead brother, in many guises, seven dead witches, a dead vicar, all your previous victims, your mother, an attack by demonic crows, some kind of poltergeist trying to throw me out of a window in my sleep, oh, and not forgetting the friendly neighbourhood Viking vampire. I mean seriously, Will, as the back door to the underworld seems well and truly off its hinges, do we really need to worry about who might come in the front?"

Eloise laughed and he laughed too and said, "Well, put like that, perhaps you have a point. But you need to sleep – no more tonight."

She became suspicious and said, "Promise me you won't look alone."

"I promise. We'll look tomorrow, if you're free."

She smiled and they turned to walk out of the maze. As they did so, Will glanced up at the roof of the school and saw a figure standing there. The figure did not try to hide himself, and though the distance was considerable, he seemed to engage Will's stare and return it, an active gaze, not that of a sleepwalker. There was no mistaking that it was Marcus Jenkins, that he'd watched them and would report their movements back to Wyndham.

Eloise didn't see him. But as they walked back, Will wondered if the time had come to silence Marcus Jenkins. Only one thing made him hesitate – the way the boy had behaved that night by the river, collecting Eloise's possessions, handing them back, apologising, the way he'd stared back from the bridge and waved. Besides, it probably wouldn't serve much purpose to kill Marcus Jenkins when the school seemed overrun with Wyndham's spies.

When they reached the school, Will stayed with Eloise as far as the staircase, but left her there.

"Tomorrow then?"

"Tomorrow, and remember to check under your bed when you go back in."

She smiled and said, "I used to do that when I was a little girl, checking for monsters."

"Don't tempt fate." He smiled as she turned and headed up the stairs.

Instead of leaving, he went from there into the entrance hall and up the main staircase. But he'd only taken a few steps before he got the scent of someone, then spotted Marcus himself on the first half-landing between floors, looking through a high window at the moonlit gardens. Will continued up the stairs cautiously, and stopped only when he had reached the same landing.

Without turning away from the window, and sounding quite calm, Marcus said, "Heading to my room? I'm not there."

"So I see."

"I knew it would be you. I just knew." He turned to face Will. It was clear he had no memory of Will being in his room. "He told me never to look into your eyes."

"So why do you?" Marcus shrugged, as if to say that he'd looked Will in the eye before so what did he have to lose. "How will you tell him, about seeing us tonight?"

"In the maze? I've already told him. I write in a book he gave me, and somehow, when I write in that book, he says it's like he can hear what I'm thinking."

So that was it, but why was he telling Will so readily about Wyndham's magic, why being so open in general? Will compared Marcus's behaviour now with the way he'd acted back in November and could only conclude that the boy sensed some connection with him. In turn, Will suspected Wyndham had underestimated the confidence and independence of this recruit.

Marcus gently rubbed the faint scar on his cheek as he thought things over. "You could kill me, I suppose. I've seen what you can do, but he'd only send someone else."

There it was again, that remarkable lack of fear Will had first witnessed down by the river. But it also seemed that Marcus didn't know there were other people in the school working for Wyndham – he imagined himself a sole spy who'd have to be replaced if he was killed.

"I could kill you, it's true . . . or you could just stop spying for him."

Marcus looked out of the window for a moment, then turned back to Will. "It's an amazing place this. I've only been here a couple of weeks and it's like my old life never happened. Books!" He laughed. "Who knew I liked books? And chess. All of it. See, I stop working for Mr Wyndham and I'll be right back where I came from, and I don't ever wanna go back to that."

Will nodded, accepting his logic, and it was odd because this boy was his adversary, but he couldn't quite treat him as an enemy. He had a strange respect for Marcus Jenkins, no less than if he was a friend playing at being an opponent, at chess, or fencing, or some other amiable pursuit.

"What do you know about the crows?"

"The dead crows?" Marcus grinned and said, "Was that you?"

Will smiled, but didn't answer and said, "Were you in Eloise's room?" Marcus shook his head, looking confused. "Promise me you won't do anything to hurt her. Spy on me all you like – just promise me that and I'll leave you alone."

Marcus looked offended that Will would even think him capable of such a thing, and said, "I'd never do anything to hurt Eloise. We're both in Dangrave House."

Will smiled again, touched by the boy's loyalty to a school house he'd belonged to for just a few weeks.

"I'm leaving now."

Marcus nodded and took that as his cue to leave too, but he stopped after climbing a few stairs and said, "Were you an Earl?"

"I still am."

Marcus smiled, bemused by this in some way, and said, "I won't tell him we spoke. It'll only make him suspicious."

He turned a second time and disappeared silently up the stairs. Will watched him go, then headed to the school office and phoned for a taxi to take him back into the city.

13

Will walked out to meet the taxi at the gates. It was after midnight and the roads were empty so he heard the car approaching from some distance, saw its lights cutting between the trees, growing in intensity.

When the driver saw Will near the gate he looked nervous, pulling to a stop and lowering his window just enough to be heard.

"You order a taxi? What name is it?"

"Wyndham, heading for the city."

The driver looked nonplussed, but gestured for Will to get in and closed his window again. "You should have waited up at the school instead of coming out in this – it's minus seven now, getting colder all the time. Reckon it could reach twelve below tonight."

"I prefer not to talk, if you don't mind."

"Suit yourself. Where are we heading?"

"Just drop me by the cathedral – it's easier for me to walk from there."

The driver shrugged, looking snubbed, and remained

silent for the rest of the journey, only occasionally giving Will a glance in the rear-view mirror. When they reached the city, Will paid him, spoke to him, left him like a person trying to remember his night's dreams.

No one was on the streets. When Will did hear voices, he turned into a street and found a church hall serving as a shelter for the night. Two people in padded jackets and woollen hats and scarves stood near the doors and smiled at Will as he passed.

One of them, a woman, gave him a little wave and said, "You're out late."

Will didn't look homeless, he supposed, but even in his overcoat he probably looked underdressed for such a cold night. It was a speculative comment from the woman, not wanting to upset him, but trying to find out if he needed a place.

"I'm fine, thank you. I'm on my way somewhere."

She smiled and said, "Take care."

Will knew this wasn't good though. The city's homeless, its runaways and vagrants, would be taking shelter for the night in this and other places. He walked street after street, finding the doorways empty.

He walked down to the old warehouse district then, where he'd found Jex and so many previous victims, knowing that there at least fires could be started and kept, and that some homeless would prefer their own fire to taking shelter in the kind of place he'd just seen.

He could feel another wave of hunger, an emptiness so complete that he felt he was outside of himself. Something deep within him screamed for blood, his thoughts falling away one by one until the scream seemed the only thing left.

But Will had underestimated the power of the cold. No one, it seemed, had chosen to stay in the open this night. He passed the gutted warehouse where he'd found Jex, continued on to the river, found the doorway in which he'd first encountered Eloise.

And here, for the first time, he picked up a human scent – it made the hunger more intense, knowing he was so close to feeding it. He walked a little further and saw him there, an old man slumped with his bags in another doorway. Will's hopes lifted and he moved quickly, but as soon as he got close he realised it was futile, that this old man had too little life left in him to satisfy Will's need for more than a few days. It hardly seemed worth it for such a short respite.

Will approached him anyway. His face and hands were blue with cold. He looked up and saw Will and smiled, his eyes looking remarkably youthful, a striking contrast to the craggy face and white beard.

Will said, "You shouldn't be out on a night like this. There's a shelter not far from here."

The man gave a little shake of his head and said in a voice that betrayed his old age, "I can't get there tonight, son."

"I'll help you. You need to be somewhere warm."

"You're a good lad, but I've no time for shelters, not tonight."

Will knew it to be true, that the old man was dying, that he would probably die even if Will carried him to the shelter. He crouched down and then sat on the step with him.

"You should get inside yourself. I'll be OK."

Will smiled and said, "I'll just stay for a little while. I'm not cold. Are you from here?"

"Hereabouts. Family's always lived here in the city or hereabouts."

"What happened?"

As cold as he was, the old man gave a mischievous grin and made a half-hearted attempt to find something. Will saw it was a bottle of cheap brandy. He took the top off and held the bottle to the old man's lips, letting him drink deep from it.

"You're a good lad," he said as Will put the bottle back. He spoke slowly, his voice weak at the edges. "Lost everything, me, a long time ago. This is what it comes to. No one else's fault, only mine. That's what it is. Yep, that's what it is."

Will looked at the old man and saw that a single tear had formed and rolled down his frozen cheek. His eyes appeared lost in some distant memory, perhaps of when life had still been full of hope for him, perhaps of the things he had lost along the way.

Will reached out and took his hand, which was as cold as his own. Just as a baby's would, the old man's fingers closed round Will's.

"You're as cold as me, lad. You should get going."

"I'm not cold." Will looked him in the eye and said, "Can I tell you a secret?" The old man didn't answer, but gave the slightest nod. "I'm nearly eight hundred years old. I'm un . . . I'm a vampire, but I'm also the Earl of Mercia by right, and you are no less my duty than all your ancestors were before you."

"I don't understand you, lad."

Will realised he hadn't made sense, and that his identity hardly mattered to this man anyway, not now.

"You don't need to understand, but what I want you to know is that this isn't the end, there is more beyond. This life is not the end of it."

The old man probably thought Will no more than a teenager with strange ideas, but he had heard his words and whatever he thought of the speaker, he sounded hopeful as he said, "You think so?"

"I do." Will stared into his eyes, capturing him now.

"Think about when you were happy, think back, your childhood, some sunny afternoon. Can you see it?"

There again, there appeared the slightest nod, and the old man smiled a little and his eyes, locked on to that faraway vision, sparkled with life, and remained like that a few minutes longer. Then for a moment his grip tightened round Will's hand before slowly releasing it as the last vestiges of life slipped away.

Will sat for a little while, thinking on the mystery of the life that had just ended before him, of all those that had come and gone before it. For a moment, his mind drifted back to a childhood afternoon of his own, but dream as he might, the cold would not claim him.

He stood again and looked about him. Such an emptiness, within and without. Nothing would come of this night to offer him sustenance, he knew that for certain. Dejected, he walked back the way he'd come and in through the city walls.

The Whole Earth was in total darkness, including those parts of the living quarters above that looked out on to the street. He thought of Chris and Rachel asleep inside, wondering whether they slept well, whether Chris's loyalty even mattered now that the focus was at Marland.

Will walked on, the floodlit cathedral spire ahead of him, its lights hazy in the frosty air. He let himself in by the side door and walked slowly up the nave, taking a seat in the front pew before the altar.

He felt at peace there, and though it didn't nourish him the way being with Eloise did, being here in this church at least tempered his hunger, enough to make it bearable for the time being. It held him fast, this place, and offered him hope.

And as he sat there beneath the illuminated dust that had so entranced Eloise, he thought back on what he'd told the old man. He'd told him there was something else, something beyond this life, and he had to believe it – had he not seen spirits? Had he not seen the spirit of his own brother, a familiarity which could not have been faked by any sorcerer?

Yet he could take no comfort from such a thought if it was true that he'd dispossessed his victims of their souls, of their very ability to experience anything beyond the lives they had led. It was a regret compounded by the knowledge that most of his victims had hardly lived the fullest or richest of lives in the first place.

Will stood up quickly, as if swift movement could help him escape such thoughts, and headed towards the crypt. He had said it to Fairburn and he believed it to be true – he would know if he carried the souls of others within him. If their souls had been imprisoned, if it was not merely another of Wyndham's tricks, then they had been imprisoned elsewhere, some place beyond his power.

Perhaps they would be released when Will uncovered his destiny, when he found Lorcan Labraid. But that thought too filled him with frustration. A notebook, a meeting with Asmund, riddles and confusions and nothing since. Where was Asmund's master? Where were the guides? Why could he not hear the call of Lorcan Labraid?

He lifted the stone between the tombs and descended, and when he reached his own chambers, he toured each of the rooms as if returning after a long absence – the pool, the empty chamber with the partly buried casket, the main room with his furniture and chests.

He opened one of the chests and took out Jex's notebook, then sat back in his chair and turned through the pages, stopping at each garbled line of prophecy. He wanted to understand, but most of all, he wanted to dream, to drift away into some sunlit afternoon as he had helped the old man to do. Only Will's sunlit afternoon was not in the past, nor in any future he could hope for.

14

Late the next afternoon, once darkness had fallen, Will made his way out of the church, pausing only to listen to the sweet chants of choral evensong being practised by the cathedral choir. No one noticed him and he left unobserved.

He made his way to the taxi rank and smiled when he realised the first car was being driven by the same man who'd brought him into the city the previous night. He looked in the rear-view mirror as Will climbed in and said, "Where to?" His face showed not even a hint of recognition.

"Marland."

"School?"

"No, the new house."

The driver started the meter and pulled away even as he said, "You sure? I don't think there's anyone there at this time of year."

"I'm sure, thank you."

"You're paying. It's funny, I was out at Marland

last night, picked up . . . who was it now? One of the teachers, I think, You're not at the school then?"

"If you don't mind, I prefer not to talk."

"Suit yourself."

They drove away from the lights of the city, the car picking up speed on the open country roads. The driver looked at Will in the mirror occasionally, just as he had the night before. Will looked at the driver too, trying not to think about how many weeks his blood might give him.

Once back at the new house, he went inside to check that nothing had gone amiss during the time he'd been away. Then, thinking forward to the night ahead, he took the sabre from the billiard room and went down to one of the cellars for a torch, conscious that it had served them well in the fight against Asmund and could again.

Even being in the cellars briefly made him grateful that he'd spent the day in his own chambers. The boredom of those cellars would have been a challenge at any time, but with his need for blood dictating his moods, it was a desperate prison. This could not continue, Will knew that – they had to make progress soon or give up.

It was still early, so he put the sword and the torch in the library and sat there for a while, watching the clock tick slowly towards a time when he might expect

Eloise to be free. Several times he considered going back into the tunnels without her, but he'd promised her he wouldn't, and he reasoned that if Wyndham was so keen to harm her, Will probably needed her more than he realised.

When he walked across to the school, she had already sneaked out and was heading towards the spot where he normally waited. She saw him and changed course slightly, walking fast as if she was about to throw her arms round him. Then, checking herself, she slowed and stopped short of reaching him.

For a moment, Will wished she had held him, even though it was always as much trial as pleasure. Instead they stood a little shy of each other, like two people still lacking the courage to say how they really felt.

Will said, "You haven't been waiting?"

"No, I just got here."

"Me too. I stayed in my chambers last night."

She looked confused for a second and he wondered if it was because he'd referred to night when he meant day, but then she said, "In the cathedral? You went into the city?" She sounded suspicious, but looked at him closely and said, "You haven't fed though."

"No."

She looked pleased, as if it had been an act of self-restraint on his part, not an absence of suitable victims.

Surely she understood that he would have to kill sooner or later, that they were unlikely to make progress fast enough to avoid it. And yet Will had to admit to himself that he had no way of knowing what they'd encounter tonight beyond the gateway, nor how close they really were to the end of all this.

They needed to press on now, but before walking away, he looked towards the Dangrave House common room. Marcus was there, deep in conversation with a boy and a girl. For once, as if they had reached some sort of understanding, Marcus did not look to the window to meet Will's gaze.

"I spoke to him last night too."

Eloise looked at the school building, struggling to see who was in the common room, then saying in disbelief, "Marcus Jenkins?"

"Yes, he was watching us the whole time we were in the maze."

"So you just had a chat? You didn't think of putting a stop to him?"

"What would you have me do? Kill him, feed off him, is that it? Do you see his death as a neat solution, an acceptable way to sate my appetites?" He was disappointed in some way, perhaps at the contrast between Eloise's comment and the boy's fierce house loyalty the previous evening.

She didn't answer at first, but she knew that had been the implication. Eventually she said, "No, I didn't mean it like that, and actually, he seems OK in a weird way. It's just that he's working against us, spying on us – you just said so yourself."

"True, and if I kill him, I'll rid the school of one spy." Will put his hands on her shoulders, giving the appearance to any watcher that they were exchanging intimacies. "Don't look now, but there's a darkened window on the top floor, the room I checked last night, a storeroom. Someone's watching us from up there right now. I can feel it, and they've been watching every evening that I've been here. What's more, I think it's the same person who drew the chalk diagrams under your bed."

"Not Marcus?"

Will shook his head. "No, he's still in the common room, and he thinks he's the only person in the school working for Wyndham. Oh, and for what it might be worth, he swore that he would do nothing to harm you."

Eloise laughed a little and said, "And you believe that?"

"As it happens, I do. Of course, everything he does could harm you indirectly, but Marcus Jenkins was not in your room."

She nodded, accepting his assurances, then said, "Well who knows, after tonight, it might not matter who's spying on us."

"We can but hope."

They set off across the parkland and Eloise said, "Did you go and see Rachel and Chris while you were in the city?"

"No, it was very late when I arrived. I just needed the solace of spending some time in my own chambers. I'm finding the cellars a trial, particularly now that my hunger has returned."

"I do think of you, you know, during the day. I think of you pacing around down there, but it must be difficult, never sleeping, day after day on your own."

"Not since I met you, though that makes the solitude even harder to bear, having something to compare it with."

"But you've had companions before, friends?"

Will shook his head. "Fleeting friendships, none quite like yours, though I met people I might have cherished had I been mortal."

"Girls?"

He thought of poor Kate who he'd seen again so recently, all the life stripped out of her, of Arabella, whom he had certainly loved in his own way.

"Yes, girls. But I've had no friendship of any kind for two centuries and more."

"Unbelievable."

"But it's true."

She laughed and said, "No, I didn't mean that, I just meant . . . it's shocking, I guess, spending year after year, twenty-four hours a day, never sleeping, never having anyone to talk to." She was sidetracked by that thought and said, "What's the longest you've ever been awake?"

"Between 1501 and . . . no, there has been one longer. I emerged from hibernation in 1813 and did not return to the earth again until 1911."

"Nearly a hundred years, that's unbelievable."

"But it's true."

Eloise realised he was teasing her this time and they both laughed, but she looked at him intently then and said, "When did you start filing your teeth?"

"I don't remember the year exactly, but many centuries ago. It was a gradual realisation that without them I looked almost normal, and that in turn would allow me to move with less suspicion about the city." It had not been enough though, Will thought, to prevent Arabella being horrified by the sight of him that night in 1742.

"Interesting. And when you . . . sorry, I don't know what's got into me. Suddenly I'm full of questions again, like I've just realised there are hundreds of things I still don't know about you."

They had rounded the stand of trees and were walking towards the new house now. Will gestured towards it.

"Perhaps you're asking because of what we're about to do, because this might be the end of it."

She held his arm, urgent as she said, "Don't say that."

"Eloise, we face dangers, both of us, and the best hope we have of seeing another day is to be prepared, to acknowledge that this might be our last." Even as he spoke, Will couldn't accept the possibility of this being Eloise's last day, much as he was prepared to accept his own fate. "I am about to attempt to open a gateway, at the very least to evil, possibly to the underworld itself, and I would think no less of you if you decided not to come with me on this part of the journey."

"Are you serious? I mean, thanks for the reality check, and I appreciate there might be bad things down there, but we're in this together, remember?" She took hold of the broken medallion hanging round her neck and held it out as if to show it to him, a movement so identical to his mother's that he stared at her in wonder. "What?"

"Nothing." She looked at him searchingly. "You just reminded me of someone else, that's all."

"Who?"

"It hardly matters – she's dead now."

"Well, that narrows it down."

Will laughed, as did Eloise, and they reached the house. They headed directly to the library where they retrieved the sabre and torch and entered the first passageway. Will opened the wall as he had before and stepped inside to the top of the steps. The lights were still on and he was about to explain to Eloise that this was part of Wyndham's trickery when he was interrupted by the sound of the wall slowly closing again behind them.

He turned and looked at it, and then responded to Eloise's expression by saying, "I've closed it myself each time previously. It didn't close on its own before."

She looked at the wall, then down the lit steps to the tunnels below. "Maybe we're expected." The first hint of nerves appeared in her eyes, but she smiled through them and held up the torch. "I've got this, you've got your sword, we've got each other, so really, what have we got to worry about?"

"Nothing."

He looked into the faultless blue of her eyes, as captured by her gaze as other people were by his. There had been other fleeting companions, it was true, but he was full of love for this girl, her beauty and her bravery, above all the sense that in some way they had always been together.

Eloise moved towards him, a little uncertain, and looked about to speak, but stopped. Will could feel her breath hot on his face. He leaned forward, fearing the worst, and kissed her lightly, his lips pressing against the softness of her mouth.

With just that briefest touch, he felt his synapses locking on to the scent of her blood, a brief twinge of pain shooting across the inside of his skull, yet it was worth it because the pain would subside, but the memory of her lips on his would sustain him.

Eloise smiled, an odd mixture of happiness and disbelief, as she said, "You kissed me." He nodded. "But . . . didn't it hurt you to do that?"

He nodded again and laughed and lied, "Not as much. Sometimes I like to think each day I spend with you I become a little more human."

"You are human, Will."

"You know what I mean. It almost feels as if, were I to spend long enough in your company, I'd become a sixteen-year-old boy again. That I'd be able to live and breathe and love you as I should. To grow old with you. It's foolish, I know."

She looked emotional and was unable to speak for a moment, but smiled and put her fingers on his cheek. Then she took a deep breath and said, "To the underworld then?"

"To the underworld."

And they started down the steps, not knowing what they would find there. Only one thing was certain, if there was a gateway, Will had to open it, no matter what lay on the other side. There was no turning back on this journey, and if he faced damnation in the hours ahead, he would take one consolation with him – he had kissed her, a simple intimacy, but one which could never be taken from him.

15

The tunnels were empty and they moved quickly. Having explored them thoroughly and then having seen the maze, Will would have been able to walk them with his eyes closed. Perhaps because of her own familiarity with the maze, Eloise was also more confident, anticipating the turns as they got to them.

And then they stopped. They had reached a junction in the labyrinth, passing from an outer circuit to an inner one, and they had turned left, only to be met by a dead end.

Eloise looked mildly puzzled as she said, "Oh, I could have sworn the passage continued this way."

"It does," said Will. "Or at least it did. This wall has been moved."

He put his hands on the stone, his palms and fingers pressing against the inscriptions and paintings that covered every part of the surface. There was nothing to suggest a mechanism inside.

"Will, this whole place looks like it's been carved out

137

of the rock, so how could a wall be moved?"

He didn't know. Perhaps the labyrinth looked carved, but had actually been constructed, like a puzzle. His mind raced through the possibilities, all of them coming back to Wyndham.

Wyndham knew from Marcus that they'd been exploring the maze. He'd no doubt realised that they now understood the labyrinth's true secret. Perhaps he also knew that they were there, with Will alerting him when he opened the wall.

And yet Wyndham was not here! If he would only show himself, Will could confront him, challenge his motives, fight him to the death if need be. But Wyndham refused to appear, and summoned the dead to fight for him, and moved walls with his remote powers, just as he'd probably shut the wall at the top of the steps.

One thing alone was in Will's favour. Wyndham had the power to intimidate, to cajole and threaten, and he had the power to frustrate, one he used to irritating effect, but he had not yet found a way of destroying Will, and until he did, Will would not be stopped.

Will turned to Eloise. "Trust me, no wall was here before. This is Wyndham's work, but he'll have to try harder than this if he's to stop us. We can still find our way through the labyrinth – it will just take a little longer."

"I agree," said Eloise, still remarkably cheerful. Was it the kiss, he wondered. Could so simple an act have made her as happy as it had made him? He could hardly believe that to be so.

They had tried to turn left and found the way blocked, so they doubled back and turned right. After another four or five turns, they found another wall that should not have been there, as if the entire labyrinth had been rotated about itself, but still they found another route and worked ever closer to the centre.

Yet despite Will's attempt to brush off the rearranged layout, there was something else troubling him. As they walked, it was as if the walls, the floor and the ceiling were all vibrating at some impossibly low frequency, not even clear enough for him to pick up, but filling the air with energy.

When they finally reached the pentagonal chamber the strange pulsating energy was obvious enough that even Eloise could feel something of it and she stared round the room, trying to locate its source. For a moment, she looked at the bronze relief on the floor and Will didn't bother to tell her that it wasn't originating from a single point, that the whole labyrinth seemed to be the source.

She pointed and said, "So the tunnel isn't dark any more."

"No, I thought I told you about the lights coming

back on." He took a couple of steps towards the tunnel, but stopped, feeling the vibrations coming up through his feet now, developing into a rumbling. He turned and looked at Eloise.

She said, "It sounds like an earthquake. I was in one once – it sounded like . . ."

She fell silent as a loud clacking noise approached rapidly, like a row of huge stone dominoes knocking one into the other. It got closer, the floor of the chamber beginning to jump with each percussive thud. Then Will heard a thundering crack and spun round to see that the tunnel to the circular chamber had closed in on itself, the two sides of the tunnel slamming together, a plume of dust filling the chamber, sparks from the severed lighting cables.

This was the only way into the chamber, he knew that much. It was unsporting of Wyndham, he thought, to let them come this far when he'd had this final trick in reserve all along. Will turned back to Eloise as the vibrations reduced once more to a background hum and the dust settled.

She was shocked, but still managed to make light of it, saying, "OK, so the walls can be moved after all. But how do we get in now?"

Will responded by walking to the point in the walls where the passage had been. He put his hands on the stone, once again reasoning that there had to be a mechanism involved. He stood there for a second and felt the stones stirring into life beneath his fingers. For a moment, he felt triumphant, but with his thoughts taking a sickening lurch, he realised he wasn't opening the tunnel up again – the walls were certainly moving, but it wasn't Will who was moving them.

"Eloise, run! Into one of the tunnels – keep running!"

He leapt backwards from the wall as it slid inwards and left. He turned, saw Eloise heeding his advice, darting into the tunnel they'd just used to get here. He started after her, but all five walls moved now, as if the pentagon was being twisted in on itself, and he realised the gaps in each of the four remaining passages were already too small for him to escape.

"Will?"

"I'm fine, keep going!"

The pentagon of the chamber seemed to twist again, the five walls sliding over each other, the pentagon becoming smaller, the earth beneath him still vibrating. Another turn of the screw, and now the walls had almost reached the hilts of the bronze swords in the floor.

There was no mistaking the intention. At some point these walls would meet, crushing him in the process. Will found himself oddly distracted by the question of whether that would kill him, or just leave him imprisoned and maimed for all eternity.

But he had his sabre in his hand. If necessary, and while he still had space, he could attempt to sever his own head, at least ending things on something resembling his own terms. It sickened him though to think that Wyndham, who as far as Will knew had no reason to hate him, would succeed in destroying him this close to what Will had hoped was the end of his journey.

"Will?"

"I'm fine," he called back, his anger building. He was angry with himself now, for always being so quick to embrace the idea of an easy death, for behaving as though Eloise meant nothing to him. He would not allow it to end like this.

The walls started to move again, and this time he ran and leapt at one of the walls as it slid towards him, planting his feet on it. The stone shuddered as he fell to the floor, another cloud of dust spitting into the room, the stones crackling and crumbling. He was swiftly back on to his haunches. The wall alongside kept moving, and for a second, a gap appeared between the two. Will didn't hesitate, diving for the opening, rolling through it, hoping only that a tunnel still lay beyond.

"Will, where are you?"

He heard the walls grinding into place behind him,

then realised the narrow tunnel he was in was also closing in on itself. He jumped to his feet, sword still in hand, and ran forward, the stones crunching together behind him, and he kept going until the section of the labyrinth he was in felt and sounded stable. He could still hear the creaking and grinding in the distance as the pentagonal chamber was consumed by its own walls.

He called out, "Eloise, I'm here. Call back to me."

He could hear a rumbling coming from elsewhere in the complex, but he was certain he could hear her voice beyond it. He walked in that direction, no longer trying to follow his memory of the maze now that it had been redesigned before their eyes – instead he walked instinctively, making turns when he needed to, heading for the sound of her.

"Call to me again!"

"I'm here!"

He walked on and after a few more minutes, he shouted, "Call . . ."

"Will, I'm here." She was close, the other side of a dead end he'd been about to walk away from.

"Thank God." The walls had stopped moving now, the energy no longer apparent, and he sighed and put his hand on the stone and said, "I'm on the other side of this wall. We're safe."

Her voice was close when she responded, and he

143

imagined her own hand pressed on the other side, almost touching his.

"I thought you'd got trapped."

"No, I'm fine. Now stay where you are and I'll find my way to you."

"You can't, Will. There's no way in. It closed around me."

"How much space have you got?"

"It's as wide as the tunnels were, and . . ." There was silence for a moment and her voice was a little more distant as she said, "About six paces long. I'm OK, but there's no way out."

He put his sabre on the floor and said, "Then I'll get you out. Stay away from this wall for now."

Will took a step back and banged his fist against the stone to test it. The wall shuddered with the impact, but it felt thick enough that he would struggle to break through using only his strength. On the other hand, he didn't want to leave her there while he went to get tools.

He looked around the edges, imagining it as a huge stone door, then noticed the smallest of gaps where it had squashed against the electric cables running along the passage it had blocked. He pushed the tips of his fingers in either side of the cable, struggling to get any kind of purchase on the stone.

The wall had been slid shut like a door and so it

would slide open again. It had to – what had been closed could always be opened. He picked up the sabre again, positioned his fingers, braced himself, pulled at the wall. It moved a fraction but nothing for the effort he'd put into it.

He heard a light humming, perhaps coming from the electric cable. He pushed his fingertips further into the gap, pulling, bracing, and as soon as the gap had opened wide enough, he rammed the hilt of the sabre into it and let go. The wall immediately tried to close the gap again, clenching tight round the hilt of the sword.

He'd be able to get both hands into the gap now, to exert more force. Of course, he didn't even know if there was a gap for this section of wall to slide into, but it had moved a little so he had to try to move it more.

The humming was louder now, and Will realised it wasn't coming from the electricity, but from the air around them, not the earth-tremor quality of the vibrations they'd heard earlier, but no less disturbing for that.

"Will, can you hear that?" Despite the slight gap in the wall, Eloise sounded more distant now.

"Yes, but don't worry, I'm nearly there."

He gripped on to the wall with both hands, put one foot up on to the adjacent wall and pulled backwards, his whole body bracing against it. He heard the sabre fall which meant the stone had to be moving, but he couldn't actually feel it.

The humming became louder, more insistent.

"Will, please hurry."

Even as he strained to pull the stone clear, at least to make a big enough gap for her to escape, he could hear her whispering to herself and he couldn't make out the words, but she sounded fearful, more so than in the whole time he'd known her.

"I'm nearly there, Eloise, everything's fine, just be ready to move when I tell you."

"But something's happening in here, Will. There's something . . ." With increasing alarm, he heard her say almost to herself, "Oh my God, what is that . . ."

Eloise screamed, no words, no call for help, just a scream, absolute terror, and the wall wasn't moving. She screamed again, and stopped. Will jumped clear of the wall and immediately it slammed back into position, the lights flickering in response, dust billowing out.

"Eloise?"

Silence.

He no longer thought of what was possible. He ran a few paces back and then hurled himself at the wall with full force. It shuddered, cracks appearing across its surface. He ran again, threw himself again, the entire tunnel shaking loose its dust and that humming still everywhere around him.

He hammered on the wall with both fists, a frenzied attack, and the cracked stone began to fall away. He hit harder, then stood back and kicked and smashed it with his fists a final time and the middle of the wall disintegrated before him in a cloud of dust and rubble.

He leapt through the gap and immediately came to a halt, a wave of relief washing over him. Eloise was at the far end, sitting on the floor, but unharmed as far as he could see, and there was nothing else in the tunnel.

Only as Will took the final few steps towards her did he realise something was very wrong. The wave ebbed away again, leaving him stranded on a foreign and frightening shore.

Eloise was staring directly ahead, as if shocked by the sight of the collapsed wall in front of her. But her eyes were locked and frozen, her face disturbingly pale and so full of fear that it had gone beyond fear and become an expressionless blank.

He knelt down in front of her, looked into eyes that did not look back, and said, "Eloise, I'm here, you're safe. Whatever you saw wasn't real."

"I saw . . ." she said, her voice still as distant as it had been from behind that wall.

"What did you see?"

But she spoke no more. Will held her face, then took her hands in his, but it was as if there was nothing responsive left within her. And his hands were inadequate, too cold to provide the comfort she needed, to reassure her that she was safe now.

What had she seen? What horror had she witnessed in those few seconds that could have reduced her to this? It was his fault, there was no denying that, not Wyndham's, but his. Will stared into her eyes, desperately hoping for some response, and he felt as if his heart, long dormant, had now been torn in two.

16

We lived like monks, Rossinière and I. Part of the cost of extended life was the abandonment of it – we led controlled, almost desolate existences, eating little, drinking less, forsaking the company of women.

Rossinière, who had lived so much longer than I, seemed hardly to notice women, though he told me he had once been married, that his wife had died in her first childbirth, together with the infant. My appetites diminished little by little, but diminish they did, for so much of the desire to eat and drink and love is born of the knowledge that we will all die. Remove that certainty and the attraction of each new dinner, each new girl becomes less and less.

Yes, we lived like monks, and watched as the world changed around us. My mother died in 1783. It was a terrible year for Europe. A volcanic eruption in Iceland filled the air with poisonous fumes and brought on a ferocious winter. My mother, as old as the century, *and already suffering a disorder of the lungs, was quick to succumb.*

Even at the end she had sent word from her deathbed that I was not to return, that my studies were more important, even though she must have believed me a man approaching conventional old age myself. I was not – I still looked no older than thirty-five, and appeared rather healthier, rather more youthful than I had when I'd first met Rossinière in the desert.

I look older now, a fit man of fifty perhaps, though I suspect I'm stronger and more agile than any normal man of thirty. In part, I look older because I am still a man, and the process of ageing is slowed but not halted. For the most part though I have aged in jolts, never fully recovering the ground lost during some shock or other. The first of these, and the greatest, took place in 1791, the year I truly understood my late mother's wisdom.

It was a tumultuous time. France was lost in the turmoil of revolution, and in the following two years the guillotine would do its work on the King and the Nobility of that country and on many others besides. The rest of the Continent was peaceful enough, but the air contained something feverish, a promise of the conflicts to follow over the next fifteen years.

Rossinière and I were in Northern Europe (it matters

not where, for the curious would find nothing now of what we found then – all I will say is that we were further north than Transylvania). We heard tales of a region that had been plagued by strange deaths, and one town in particular, which had witnessed five bloodless corpses within the space of two years.

Such was our curiosity for the world that we were bound to investigate, but I must confess that I did not link these mysterious deaths in any way with the quest which had governed my life for nearly half a century.

It was a remote region of mountains and forests, the town containing no more than five thousand people in huddled and picturesque streets (no doubt my memory has erased the smell and the squalor – I have been back to that town in the last half-century and it is considerably larger, but also much cleaner than it was then).

There was an inn of sorts, but the local nobleman welcomed us into his castle and was eager for us to make use of his library – we gratefully accepted and pretended to find knowledge there that we didn't already possess.

When we told him the purpose of our journey, we thought he might respond with exasperation at the backwardness of his subjects, their superstitions and nonsensical beliefs. Instead he responded with the utmost relief, as if we had been sent by God to deliver him and his people from the evil that persecuted them.

For this nobleman – and I am purposefully avoiding his name in this – was convinced not only that the murderer was to be found somewhere within his castle, but that it was in fact some ancestor of his.

"Your ancestor?" Rossinière's thoughts leapt ahead and he said, "Am I to understand you think a vampire responsible for these murders?"

I had heard the term before during our travels, but had never thought more of it than a backward superstition. Perhaps Rossinière had thought the same because he seemed both astonished and full of anticipation as he awaited an answer.

The nobleman nodded sadly and said, "It sounds ridiculous to say so in an age of science, but I do believe that, for two reasons. The first is that I've studied the private papers of my family over the last three centuries and this same plague has occurred repeatedly, claiming victims for years on end, disappearing for decades, only to return again, and in the papers of both my grandfather and his grandfather, there are comments suggesting a mysterious figure had been seen repeatedly within the castle. That would be reason enough in itself."

"But you have a second reason," I said.

"Yes, perhaps more compelling than the first." He stood and said, "Gentlemen, if you would accompany me to the crypt, there is something there I'm certain you'll find of interest."

By candlelight, he led us down into the castle's crypt and there showed us the tomb of one of his ancestors, a man who'd died at the beginning of the fifteenth century at the age of twenty-eight. He'd been on a military campaign, had fallen sick with a fever and died shortly after. His body had been brought home and laid to rest.

Rather than call his servants, the nobleman had us help him remove the stone lid from the tomb. An empty casket lay within, the lid resting to the side of it.

"The lid of the casket is the real key," he said, and had us lift it clear with him.

Rossinière and I stared at it in a state of wonder. The one appetite we had never lost was curiosity, the thirst for more knowledge, and this coffin lid spoke of knowledge even we had not yet discovered.

The inside was badly scratched, the unmistakable scars left by sharpened fingernails. This in itself would have been merely a curio, for it's sad to say that the accidental burial of living people was not so very uncommon at that time.

But the coffin lid was also split, despite the thickness of the wood, and the damage had apparently been made by a heavy blow from the inside, as if the buried man had punched the lid free. The fierceness of the blow that *would have been required to break out of such a solidly built casket was plain for us all to see.*

After a moment's silence, Rossinière said, "How was this discovered?"

"The first attack took place thirty years after his death. At the time, the daughter of the house dreamt again and again of this tomb so her father had it opened. It was found to be empty, just as I've shown you now."

"But the lid of the tomb had been replaced," I said.

"Exactly. There was no damage to the tomb itself, so I can only presume that once free of his coffin, he was more careful in removing the stone above him, and he was certainly careful in replacing it afterwards. There have been no signs that he has ever returned to it."

Rossinière tapped the edge of the open casket and said, "In the stories I have heard, these creatures sleep by day and live by night, but the timings you give suggest something very different. Is it not possible that they hibernate for many years at a time, then are active for similar periods? If so, then somewhere within this castle right now, somewhere hidden beyond the eyes of your family and servants, your ancestor is active."

The nobleman smiled and said, "My family, as you may have noticed, is absent – I sent them to stay with my wife's brother."

"Has anyone within the castle itself ever been a victim?"

"Many years ago, one of the serving girls. The family has been spared, and I like to believe that even possessed by demons my ancestor respects the family line, but I would rather not tempt fate where my own children are concerned."

Of course, I know now why his ancestor spared him and his family. In part it would have been an act of self-preservation – if a nobleman's wife had been slain, he might have torn the castle apart in search of the demon. But the noblemen themselves, and their children, had been spared for a simpler reason.

These demons cannot breed, but this cannot always have been so because I know now that some people carry the vampire bloodline within them. If bitten, it is these people who return as demons. And it seems these same people provide no sustenance to the vampire because they are rarely, if ever, chosen as victims. This is why the demon in the castle spared the noble family, because their blood offered him nothing, except possible companionship.

For three days we searched every corner of the castle, but found no hiding place. Nevertheless, we came to certain conclusions. Though we couldn't find it, we sensed his hiding place had to be underground, all the better to remain undetected through the long years of his hibernations. During his waking years we reasoned he would want to leave the castle undetected as often as he chose. And through a process of elimination we reasoned that there was one internal courtyard he was most likely to cross as he made his way from the cellars to the outside world.

The next night we took a position in a tower high above the courtyard. The kitchen was below us and Rossinière reasoned that the smell of foodstuffs would prevent the demon from picking up our scents. There was a waxing half-moon in a clear sky, so our eyes were also quick to adjust to the gloom.

It served no purpose, for no one appeared in the courtyard. We slept the following day and returned as darkness fell. This time our patience was rewarded.

No sooner had the night established itself than a figure slipped across the courtyard. We lost sight of it quickly, and assumed it had made for the castle gates. Just as we were waiting to hear them open, I spotted the shadow of the demon again – it had leapt up on to the castle walls and now bounded over them as easily as a cat might have scaled a garden wall.

He was gone, but we waited, and four hours later we saw him reappear in the same place and return across the courtyard. Both of us knew that he must have leapt the height of six men or else scaled a sheer wall. It would take all of our acquired powers and more to match such a demon as this.

There was no attack that night, so sensing that the demon didn't restrict himself to wandering when he needed to feed, we decided we would set a trap each night until he reappeared.

"They fear light and crucifixes," said Rossinière. "We'll arm ourselves of course, but light and crucifixes will be our greatest weapons."

The following night, some of the castle's trusted servants were positioned behind the doors that opened on to the courtyard, each with a torch soaked in oil and a candle with which to light it. Rossinière, the nobleman and I were all fully armed and hidden in different locations to maximise our chances of seeing the demon as he stepped into the courtyard.

We didn't expect him to come two nights in a row, but come he did, and I can only presume in retrospect that the demon suffered boredom as much as any of us. He emerged from a doorway and took a few steps across the courtyard before coming to a stop.

He lifted his face to the air, as if able to smell that something was wrong. He seemed torn as to whether he should proceed or turn back, but then Rossinière's cry rang through the courtyard, "Now!"

The nobleman and I emerged from our hiding places, as did Rossinière, so that we were surrounding the demon to some degree. For one tense moment nothing else happened but then doors opened all around us and the courtyard suddenly blazed with the light of the burning torches.

The violent change hurt my eyes so I had a certain sympathy for the demon as he screamed in pain in the centre of the courtyard. My vision adjusted, but his did not and even as he tried to observe what was happening around him, he continued to grimace and squint against the glare.

We had the chance to observe him and he was something to behold, wearing the clothes of an earlier age, but looking as strong and healthy as the young man he'd been. What was more, the family resemblance was obvious, so much so that the nobleman looked astounded by his appearance.

As the demon calmed somewhat, still shielding his eyes but looking dangerous now, ready to strike out at his persecutors, Rossinière stepped forward brandishing a large gold crucifix. The demon backed away from him until he was against a wall, and there, in limited shadow, he finally opened his eyes.

Rossinière continued to press him until he stood immediately before the demon, holding him at bay with

158

the crucifix. He shouted, "Don't look into its eyes – I see it has some mesmerising power."

He stared himself though – Rossinière and I had already developed our own powers beyond the point of being caught up in the demon's hypnotic spell.

Yet Rossinière had counted too much on the knowledge of others, based as it was upon half-truths and superstition. Just as he seemed to have the demon under his control, the creature smiled, revealing its unsightly fangs, then pulled the crucifix from Rossinière's hand and kissed it before saying, "What have I to fear from this?"

Without looking, he threw the crucifix away, sending it spinning across the courtyard and impaling one of the servants in the chest. The servant let out a single shocked cry and fell with his burning torch. Another servant dropped his torch at the sight of it and ran from the courtyard.

Rossinière made for his sword, but the initiative was lost, and I heard a terrible cracking noise and saw Rossinière's body hurtle across the courtyard where it slammed against the castle wall and fell like a broken doll.

For a moment, none of us knew what to do, and I was rendered incapable by the sight of Rossinière's lifeless body, a man who'd been the best of brothers to me for the last twenty-five years, killed in a careless instant.

The demon turned to the nobleman and started slowly towards him, saying, "That you, of all people, would conspire with these villains to undo me. Do family ties mean nothing to you, nor all our shared history?"

The nobleman could not answer and looked distraught, as if he feared he had indeed betrayed his own flesh and blood. I was pulled back from my grief though by curiosity, by hearing the demon talk of family loyalty, of villains, as if he were still very much the man he'd once been. Not that I doubted for a second that he would kill his noble descendant as readily as he would kill the rest of us if it suited his needs.

He was still walking towards the nobleman, but I glanced one more time at Rossinière and did not hesitate. I drew my sword and grabbed a flaming torch from a servant who stood nearby. We had been wrong about the crucifix, but I had seen the pain caused by light or fire.

The demon knew it too. He lunged forward and pulled the sword from the nobleman's sheath, thrusting him to one side, almost as if wishing to push him out of harm's way. He turned and drew a fast stroke through the air, but I responded by swiping the flaming torch at him. He jumped back and I stepped into his retreat and drove my blade into his body.

160

The demon closed his eyes against the torch which was now at my side, but he held the blade where it entered his body and struck out with his own sword, a shattering blow which left only a flesh wound, but which, I later found, had broken my shoulder. In shock, I dropped the torch, but it fell towards him and he jumped back, his body pulling free of the sword as if it had left no injury.

I knew he was fast and strong so even as pain seared through my shoulder, I kicked the fallen torch towards him and the flames leapt at his clothes as if finding dry tinder, immediately engulfing him. He let out a bellowing scream and swung his sword furiously at the torch, but seemed momentarily frozen to the spot in shock or pain.

I could not be sure the flames would be enough, even with that terrible scream filling the air and the fire eating up his clothes and flesh, and so I did what instinct told me to do. With my good arm, I swung my sword as hard as I could muster and struck his neck.

Silence followed, and a brief dazzling blue light, and the nobleman's sword clattered to the floor as the flames died back to the fallen torch. Nothing of the demon remained, nothing whatsoever. I saw him disappear, even as I rested my sword on the floor like a walking cane, as I fell slowly next to it, then slipped into unconsciousness.

There was so much still to learn of the world, but I would have to learn it alone. Rossinière was dead. And when I woke the next day, bandaged and nursed, my shock was as great as the nobleman's must have been, for I'd aged ten years and I never really got those years back.

Word of what I had done spread amongst the nobility of the region and I sought out and destroyed other vampires over the next several years, each time getting stronger, learning more, developing my own black arts that I might be still better equipped to destroy this evil.

Yet even as I fought and did what I believed to be my duty, I knew a greater duty was demanded of me. Back in the early years of that century I was now certain my mother had encountered a vampire. And now, at the century's end, I knew the time had come to return home and complete the journey on which she had set me all those years before.

17

Eloise was able to sit on one of the sofas in the library, but Will had still failed to get any further response from her. He'd put on one small lamp, but Eloise stared ahead as if blind to everything around her, not blinking, registering nothing.

Will heard a car approaching, coming to a stop on the gravel outside; he heard their voices and the light knocking on the main door. He didn't want to leave her at all, and not just because of the fragile state she was in, but because he still couldn't be sure that Wyndham's attacks had ceased.

He had no choice though, and crouched in front of her, saying, "I'll be back in a moment. I'll be able to hear if you call." Her eyes stared through him.

He walked quickly through the house and opened the door. It had been the only choice, the only thing he could think of, and ironically, he had never been happier to see them. Chris and Rachel stood there, both looking equally concerned.

Chris stepped through the doorway first, saying, "What's happened?"

"Please tell me she's not hurt," said Rachel.

Will closed the door and said, "She's not hurt, not physically. Do you need more light or can you see well enough?"

"We're fine," said Chris.

"Then follow me. I don't want to leave her alone."

As they walked, Will explained briefly what had happened. And when they reached the library, they stopped together just inside the doorway, all looking at Eloise where she sat on the sofa, as blank as the ghosts of Will's victims had been.

Rachel said, "She hasn't said anything at all since it happened?"

"She said, 'I saw', but couldn't tell me what, and has said no more since."

Rachel walked across to Eloise and the others followed. She knelt down in front of her, took her hands, looked into her eyes. Will noticed Eloise's hands holding on to Rachel's, responding to her touch in a way they had failed to do to his. This is why he'd called Rachel and Chris, because she needed people with human warmth, people who could coax her back, but it only served to remind him again of how inadequate he was.

Rachel's voice was almost a whisper as she spoke to

Eloise. Will and Chris looked on, then Rachel turned to them and said, "It might help if the two of you left us alone for a little while. Let me talk to her."

Chris looked around the room as if to ask where they could go, but Will said, "Come, I'll show you where it happened."

It didn't matter now if Chris was working in Wyndham's interests. The sorcerer already knew everything and more of what Will knew. Perhaps too, if Chris saw Wyndham's determination to hurt Eloise, it might make him question his allegiances.

That was all on the assumption that Chris *had* betrayed him. If he hadn't, showing him the tunnels would reinforce in his mind that Will trusted him. And Will did want to trust him because this incident had proved that his own powers were unlikely to be enough on their own.

They entered the first secret passage and found the wall to the second still open. Chris hesitated, looking at the steps.

Will went first and said, "Come."

Chris followed him, along the tunnel and into the labyrinth proper where he immediately stalled, poring over the inscriptions and pictures that covered the walls. Will didn't slow down, but hesitated at each turn or junction to ensure Chris was still behind him.

"This is incredible," said Chris, his interest in the paranormal taking over. "From an archaeological point of view of course, but in terms of the occult, this could add so much to the field of knowledge."

Will didn't respond directly, but said, "Look how solid these walls are, how the tunnels appear to be carved out of the rock itself, yet walls moved down here, blocking off tunnels, closing in on chambers. They moved as easily as you might open and close a door. Wyndham did that, I'm certain of it."

Chris looked uneasy, perhaps only concerned that his expression shouldn't make him look guilty when he wasn't, and he said, "You think he's been attacking her?"

"I know he has – the witches told me as much. Three times so far, each different, each equally disturbing. And I fear he hasn't finished with her yet."

Chris looked astounded and said, "Once again, if the Wyndham I met is the same person, and I still find that unlikely . . ."

"It's him," said Will. "However unlikely, it's him."

"But the person I've met just doesn't seem capable of things like that – I don't mean the magic, I mean attacking a defenceless girl."

"Have you seen him since we spoke?"

"No. As it happens, I contacted Breakstorm after that because I wanted to meet him again, knowing what you'd said about him, but they told me he was away."

"Busy perhaps, but not away." They turned a corner and Will pointed ahead to the demolished wall. He knew his own strength and yet still he was surprised to see the damage he had inflicted in his desperation. "This is where he trapped her, beyond that wall. I only wish I knew what she saw in there, what he made her see."

Chris approached and stared across at the small chamber from the edge of the broken wall, apparently nervous of stepping inside. Then he looked at the wall itself.

"You broke through this?" Will nodded. "Wow."

"You can climb through the gap – it's stable enough."

Chris started to shake his head slowly and said, "I'll pass on that, I think. I don't know what it is, but there's a strange atmosphere in there, something . . . I don't know, but something sinister."

Will stepped over the broken wall and looked around, putting his hands on the stone here and there, and said, "I don't feel anything." It was true now that he thought of it; the previously uncomfortable atmosphere that had filled the labyrinth had disappeared.

"Maybe I'm just giving myself the creeps, but something definitely feels wrong down here." Chris looked down at the rubble. "Couldn't you just smash your way through to wherever the gateway is?"

"I could. But I would probably complete Wyndham's mission for him by burying myself in rubble. He has moved these walls around so comprehensively that I would have to destroy half the labyrinth before finding the chamber I need, if indeed anything remains of it – we saw the walls close in on one chamber until it disappeared completely."

Will stepped back through, saw his sabre where it had fallen on the floor and picked it up. Idly, he inscribed shapes in the dusty floor.

"If there's a gateway, and if that gateway leads where I hope it does, I must find another way to access it."

Chris put his hand on the wall nearest him as if to test how solid it was, and said, "But you said yourself, you can't get back to where it was."

Will smiled. "This gateway is not, as far as I can tell, a physical thing – it is something else entirely. If it is tied to a physical place, then you're right, we have no choice but to find a way back through the labyrinth."

Will hadn't given up on the labyrinth yet, but he doubted Wyndham would have left anything to chance given the enormous forces he had deployed in moving these walls. But he would explore further once he was on his own again.

He was still treating Chris and Rachel with caution, but Chris confused him even further by suddenly becoming enthusiastic as he said, "We could go in from above! The ley lines come together here, so maybe that's over the gateway you're talking about. All we have to do is find the central point of that triangle, which has to be in the abbey ruins somewhere, then we dig down and find the chamber you were looking for."

Will was impressed in some way, not by the optimistic leaps and assumptions, but by Chris's enthusiasm, by his determination to find a solution to a problem that was not really his. But if Will had learned one thing over the centuries, it was patience.

"It's worthy of consideration, but digging up the grounds of an ancient monument might bring more attention than we would want."

"I hadn't thought of that."

Nevertheless, Will smiled and said, "We'll think of something. But we should go back to the others."

They made their way back to the library and this time Will closed the wall at the top of the steps. Rachel looked up when they came in, but her expression suggested she was at a loss as to what to do. Eloise still sat staring blankly in front of her.

"I think we should get her to a doctor."

Chris said, "I don't see how that will help. There doesn't seem to be anything physically wrong with her."

Rachel looked into Eloise's eyes, then back to Chris

and Will. "No, but she's traumatised in some way, beyond anything we can do for her."

"Traumatised by something that's also beyond the knowledge of the medical profession."

"Chris, she's a young girl, with a family who need to know what's happened to her."

"She has no family," said Will. "Only me."

He'd said it before he realised what he was saying, but Rachel didn't question his words and merely said, "Then what do you think we should do?"

"She needs to be kept safe, and she needs to rest. If rest doesn't bring her back to herself, then you may be right, but I fear if she doesn't come back to us of her own accord, no doctor will be of help."

"OK, we'll take her back to our place for now." Will was about to object, but Rachel said, "Where else can she go?"

He had thought to take her back to his chambers beneath the church, but it made sense now that he thought of it; she would be better with them, in the warmth, somewhere that she would be less likely to be haunted by whatever it was she had seen.

"You must promise me that one of you will stay with her at all times."

"Of course," said Chris.

Rachel said, "What about the school – we don't

want them thinking she's gone missing again."

Will thought back to his wanderings around the school in the hours he'd spent waiting for Eloise to appear. Several times he'd stared in at the headmaster working in his study, long after his secretary had left, usually while the rest of the school was at dinner. It would be easy, Will thought, to speak to the headmaster without being seen by anyone else, to plant in his thoughts some memory of Eloise visiting family.

"I'll deal with the school. And I will come to you tomorrow evening."

"We can pick you up."

"No, you stay with Eloise." As an afterthought, he said, "But how will you do that? You have your establishment to run."

Chris looked about to speak, but Rachel said, with no room for argument, "No, the café stays closed tomorrow."

It was decided. Will carried Eloise to their car and watched as they drove away towards the city with her. She had to get better, there was no other possibility. She had to get better because without her he was defeated, in every way.

18

Will spent the rest of the night and all of the daylight hours in the tunnels. There was peace and calm down there now, no sense of the tectonic shifts that had taken place earlier, no sense of brooding disquiet. He wondered if the change in atmosphere had come about because these tunnels no longer led to the gateway he'd sought.

That seemed likely. On his own he was able to rebuild an image in his mind of how the labyrinth had been rearranged, and within the first hour, he could tell that there was no longer any way of even getting close to the site of the circular chamber.

It didn't stop him looking, or calculating how many walls he might have to knock through to reach a gateway that could have been demolished anyway. He didn't see how it could be done, particularly when Wyndham probably had it within his power to set the walls moving all over again.

Just before darkness fell the following afternoon,

he spent a little time in the one tunnel he'd otherwise avoided, where Eloise had been trapped. It puzzled him and made him angry again, wondering what had happened to her in there. He'd come close to admiring Wyndham, this unseen adversary, but he was determined now of one thing – he would destroy the sorcerer, or be destroyed in the process.

He didn't linger once he'd left the tunnels, but headed directly to the school. Instead of approaching in the normal way, for his prime spot in front of the Dangrave common room, he walked round the back of the building and cut along in its own shadows until he was able to look from a small shrubbery into the headmaster's study.

He was sitting there now, a slim, sporty man in his forties. On a shelf on the far wall there were some trophies, which Will imagined were his, some for running, others for tennis. His hair was receding, but it was cut short enough so as not to make too much difference. He had a clipped military bearing somehow, a look that seemed out of place with what Eloise had told Will about the school.

A secretary came into the office, but even without Will being able to hear the brief conversation, it was clear she was saying goodnight, that her working day was over. The headmaster smiled and went back to his paperwork.

Over the next ten minutes the headmaster didn't stir and nor did Will. He heard a few cars driving away from the other side of the property, could smell food and hear the general good-humoured clatter of the school having dinner.

Will made his way inside then, through a door nearby which allowed the headmaster access to his own private shrubbery garden. He walked past the two darkened administrative offices, into the small hallway where visitors and students were kept waiting.

He looked at the nameplate on the door: Dr Paul Higson.

Will knocked on the door and opened it without waiting for a response. The headmaster looked up as if annoyed that someone should come in without being summoned first, but he saw Will and smiled awkwardly.

"Just a moment, please – I'll just finish reading this paragraph."

"Of course," said Will. He closed the door behind him and walked across to stand in front of the desk.

The headmaster pored intently over the document in front of him, a pen poised in his hand. It would be quick, Will imagined – hypnotise him as soon as he looked up from his paperwork, fill his head with thoughts of Eloise going to visit a sick relative, remind him that he'd forgotten to inform the other staff members. If it didn't work perfectly, it would work well enough to make Eloise's new absence less problematic.

The headmaster put his pen down and said, "Just a second and I'm with you." He was still looking closely at the document, and for the first time, Will became suspicious. It seemed odd that anyone in the headmaster's position would so resolutely fail to make eye contact with a visitor, a stranger at that, someone who was not a student of the school, but appeared to be of that age.

Higson reached into the drawer at the side of his desk, saying, "Just staple these together and I'm done."

Will glanced at the stapler sitting on the desk next to Higson's telephone, but it was too late. Higson pulled a small but powerful torch from the drawer. He pushed himself backwards at the same time as he turned on the torch and directed its beam straight at Will's eyes.

He said, "Stay back, get away from me!"

The pain was immediate and dazzling, ripping through Will's eyes with a power that felt as if it might tear his skull apart. He was as stunned by his own stupidity as much as by the torch beam – obviously Wyndham had a connection with the school, obviously he'd had more than one person there working for him, so why hadn't it occurred to Will that the headmaster himself might be in league with the sorcerer?

He was furious too, because this man was supposed to be concerned with Eloise's welfare, but was actually part of a vicious plan to harm her. Higson was as guilty as Wyndham for the state Eloise was in now, perhaps more so given his duty of care.

The fury seethed up inside Will until he could no longer feel the pain, and though he couldn't see, his other senses told him exactly where Higson was. Will threw the desk to one side and lunged forward. He grabbed Higson by the shirt and tie and threw him up against the wall with so much force that a painting fell to the floor nearby.

Higson let out a cry of alarm and tried to redirect the torch beam into Will's eyes. Will grabbed his hand and crushed it instantly around the torch. The torch dropped to the floor and Will stood on it, smashing it.

Will's vision was coming back to him now and he looked up into Higson's face. Higson was kicking and flailing at Will, becoming more fearful with the growing realisation that his strength was inadequate. All Higson could do was avoid Will's gaze and he did this by turning his head frantically to the side, exposing his neck.

Will looked at the vein throbbing above Higson's collar, but he was too angry even to think about blood for the moment. Instead he lowered Higson to the floor while keeping him pinned to the wall, and now that they were on the same level, he grabbed Higson's face with his free hand and turned it forcibly to face him.

Higson closed his eyes and was whimpering now, all his military bearing gone, to the extent that Will no longer believed he had ever been a soldier.

"Open your eyes and look at me."

"Never."

"Then I'll rip off your eyelids."

"Please, don't, I . . ."

"I have no intention of hypnotising you. But I tell you again, I will rip off your eyelids unless you open them. Wyndham has surely told you that I come from an age when such a torture would have been considered rather mundane."

"I . . ."

"Open them!"

Higson opened his eyes, blinked them shut again, twice, and finally opened them properly, revealing them to be full of tears and terror.

"I was going to hypnotise you, but not now. Not now that I know you work for Wyndham."

"I haven't done anything."

"Eloise is in your care, yet you have allowed Wyndham to conspire to do her harm – you consider that nothing? You allow him to fill the school with his spies – you consider that nothing?"

"But I haven't, please believe me. Marcus Jenkins, he's the only . . . what I mean is, he's the only connection with Wyndham. I haven't conspired, I swear it."

"Then your oath is worthless. You avoided eye contact, you used light to attack me, things you would not know if you were not in Wyndham's trust. Reverend Fairburn was the same before you and he, let me remind you, is dead. So ask yourself where your fear should lie, with Wyndham, or with me?"

Higson winced with pain, and looked panicked and distraught as he said, "I think my hand's broken."

"Three fingers and the knuckle of your middle finger, not even a hint of the pain and injury I could inflict upon you." The pain behind Will's own eyes had almost subsided now, and he said, "Eloise has gone away for a day or two. You'll tell staff that you knew about it, that she's gone to visit a sick relative. You won't question her when she returns, nor will you speak to her."

Higson nodded, eager to comply.

"I had planned to make you follow these instructions by hypnotising you, but I want you to be conscious of what I've told you because I want you to understand something else. If any harm comes to Eloise, whether you are directly responsible or not, neither Wyndham nor anyone else will be able to protect you – mark this, I will look upon it as a point of honour that her suffering is returned to you tenfold."

"I understand."

Will let him go and stepped away from him. Higson immediately clutched his injured hand, tentatively daring to look at the extent of the injuries. Will looked at the desk, solid and imposing, and casually pulled it upright again, leaving the debris lying on the floor.

He crossed the room to the door, but stopped and looked around briefly, then said, "My family built this house."

Despite his wounded hand and his earlier terror, Higson produced an unconvincing expression of defiance as he said, "You're a vampire – you don't have a family."

Will smiled. "I stand corrected. My brother's family built this house."

Higson looked bewildered, but said, "Yes, yes, I know that."

"Good."

Will left by the same door and headed back across the park to the new house. He would call a taxi from there. He had no family, not any more, but he had described Eloise as his family earlier, and it was true in one sense at least, because she was the first person in over seven centuries for whom he would be prepared to die, and the first for whom he would be prepared to kill in anger. His words to Higson had been a promise, and not intended for Higson alone.

19

As Rachel had promised, The Whole Earth was closed for the day and Will couldn't make himself heard at the front of the property. He made his way to the back and as he walked past the kitchen window, Chris saw him and waved, then came to the door to let him in.

As he opened the door, he met Will's concerned expression with a smile and said, "She's fine. Rachel's with her. She slept all night and most of today, then woke a couple of hours ago and she's been talking."

"The trauma has left her?"

Chris looked hesitant, but said, "It's early days. I think she'll recover, but she still looks . . . I don't know, like someone recovering from a fever or something, you know, like she's had the stuffing knocked out of her."

"May I go up?"

"Of course. She's in the guest room – you'll probably hear Rachel."

Will walked through and climbed the stairs, picking

181

up Rachel's voice immediately, then perhaps a single word from Eloise. As he got closer he could hear Rachel more clearly, saying, "Oh, this was a favourite of mine . . ."

She started to read, poetry – Byron, he thought. He stood outside the door and listened as she finished, lulled by Rachel's beautiful, slightly musical reading voice.

Will knocked and opened the door. He couldn't help notice, and was stung by it, that Eloise recoiled in fear for just a moment before realising it was him and smiling.

She was sitting up in bed in borrowed nightclothes. Rachel was sitting on the bed next to her. There was a chair beside the bed and Will walked over and sat on it as he said, "You're feeling better?"

Eloise smiled again, but looked groggy as she said, "I don't know that I've been ill. I just feel like I've woken up after a really long sleep, like I'm still only half awake."

"You had a terrible shock," said Rachel. "But your mind's probably blocking it – that's why you feel confused." She stood up, leaving the anthology of poetry behind as she said, "I'll go and make that tea."

She left the room and Eloise said, "Chris said you saved me."

"Not really, and I shouldn't have endangered you in

the first place. You were trapped, that was all, and I broke down the wall to get you out."

He suddenly realised she was making as little eye contact with him as one of Wyndham's disciples. But she turned and looked at him directly now as she said, "I remember what I saw, Will. I haven't told Rachel and Chris because it'll just confuse them and make them suspicious. But I do remember."

"Make them suspicious? But why, what did you see?"

"I saw you, Will, I saw you." Her eyes were pleading now, wanting him to reassure her in some way, but he couldn't imagine how seeing him might have traumatised her like that.

"I was on the other side of the wall, you know that. Anything you saw inside that chamber wasn't real, it was created by Wyndham. If he showed me dead or injured, that's just his attempt to weaken you."

"No, it wasn't that. You weren't hurt. I mean . . ." It looked for a moment as if the vision had flashed back into her memory and she had to steel herself before continuing. "I know it was probably Wyndham's work, and I know I should ignore it because it's lies, but it looked so real, felt real. It was you as you'll become, when you achieve your destiny. And it was frightening, really frightening."

"It was a lie," said Will. "He knows nothing of me or

my destiny, and you will never have reason to be afraid of me."

"I know that."

How could she know that? She had known him weeks and had seen only the better part of him. She wanted to believe in him, he understood that much, but something of what she'd seen in those tunnels had shaken her belief.

Will shook his head, and said, "No, you don't know that, neither of us do – how can I know what my destiny will mean for me? What will become of me? If you saw me a devil, then perhaps a devil is what I will become."

"That's impossible," she said, suddenly full of conviction.

"It is possible – if it was not, you wouldn't have been so disturbed by the vision he put before you. It serves neither of us to pretend it couldn't happen – vigilance is the only way of ensuring that it doesn't." Eloise looked downcast, but then he said, "Wyndham has already tried to harm you, and now he has tried to poison your thoughts, as he will no doubt do again. The only thing I ask is that you think on the witches. Have they not always put your interests first? They didn't want you to go to Puckhurst, remember? They alerted me to the attempt on your life just the other night. They have questioned my loyalty too, but have they ever warned you to stay away from me?"

Eloise smiled and looked up, reaching at the same time for her pendant, panicking when she realised it was gone. She looked on the bedside cabinet, on the bedclothes around her.

"Where's my pendant? Did I lose it in the tunnels?"

"Not that I remember." He heard Chris and Rachel coming up the stairs and along the landing, and as they came into the room, Eloise looked ready to jump out of bed in a frenzy.

"What happened to my pendant, do you know?"

Rachel was carrying a tea tray. She smiled and said, "Don't worry, I've got it. You were having some sort of nightmare while you were sleeping and you tore it off. I put a new leather strap on it."

She put the tea tray down on the bed and crossed the room to a tall, narrow chest of drawers. She opened the top one, took the pendant out and brought it back to Eloise.

Eloise looked at it, checking nothing was wrong, then slipped it back over her head. She looked immediately relieved to be wearing it again, the significance of having torn it from her neck apparently passing her by.

Will understood the action perfectly. He'd described Wyndham as having tried to poison her thoughts, and realised now that he'd already succeeded. Yes, Eloise had come back to him, the attack had not been fatal to their relationship, but a small stubborn residue of that poison remained, just enough that it would be harder for her to be certain of him in future. She didn't know it, but she would be always watchful, looking for signs of the evil that might be within him.

Chris was standing at the bottom of the bed and now he said, "You're looking much better. How do you feel?"

Eloise smiled, once again a schoolgirl, embarrassed by all the fuss. "I feel fine, honestly. I'll go back tomorrow, if that's OK with you. I mean, I don't want you to close the café or anything."

"Not at all. When do you want to go back?"

"In the morning?"

"Well, we don't open until ten, so we could take you back before that without having to close."

"Great." She smiled, and glanced awkwardly at Will. He knew what she'd done, choosing to return in daylight, and could hardly blame her for wanting to go back without him. He smiled back, letting her know that it didn't matter, that he understood. She looked helpless and a little ashamed in response, but he could offer her no other reassurance.

Rachel said, "What about you, Will? When can we take you back?"

"Please, don't worry about me. I have some things to attend to here in the city. I'll go back late tomorrow night, but I'll take a taxi – one driver in particular is becoming quite used to me."

They laughed, and so did Eloise in a distracted way, and she looked surprised when Will stood.

"In fact, I will need to go now." He reached for Eloise's hand, but she instinctively withdrew it. Then she caught herself and held him, her fingers warm, a warmth which had made him feel alive, but which now made him feel all the more dead and frozen. "I'll be back too late to see you tomorrow, I suspect, but the next night?"

"Of course."

He nodded and Chris said, "I'll see you out."

As they walked down the stairs, Will said, "Try, if you can, to find out where Wyndham lives. He's a mortal man, whatever his powers, so he must live somewhere."

"I'll try, but he seems to be an expert at keeping under the radar."

"Perhaps if you check which buildings are owned by The Breakstorm Trust – he might use that as a way of concealing where he lives."

"I'll do that. You're sure you don't want a lift tomorrow night? If it's late, the café will be closed anyway."

"It might be even later than that, but I prefer to go

alone when I can – I will no doubt call on you enough in the months ahead."

Chris nodded, and then as they reached the back door, he said, "Don't take it personally. You know, Eloise being a bit awkward around you all of a sudden – she's had a shock, that's all." Will smiled and Chris laughed as he said, "Of course, how stupid – I'm giving relationship advice to someone who's seven hundred years older than me."

"Not stupid at all," said Will. "Goodnight to you."

And he left and walked the streets for a little while before heading to the cathedral. It was cold again and the shelter was recruiting – he saw the same young woman who this time offered him a friendly wave, but didn't speak. Perhaps it was less cold and there would be potential victims, but he did not want to feed; he wanted the hunger to consume him.

There was destiny, and the centuries of leading up to this point, but Will couldn't help but think that the best thing for Eloise would be if he took to the earth now and rose again after she'd died. Yes, her own destiny might be thwarted in the process, but she would lead a short, happy life and marry someone and have children, and remember these past weeks as if they'd been a dream.

But he could not go back to the earth, it wasn't within his power to choose, and so he would keep going until this had come to a conclusion of one kind or another. He would spend the rest of the night and the following day in his chambers.

He'd go back to Marland as soon as it got dark. He'd told her otherwise only to excuse her the obligation of having to meet him that evening. Nor did he want to meet with Eloise. If he wanted to talk to anyone now, it was Marcus Jenkins.

20

He didn't have the taxi drive him up to the new house but had him stop on the road nearby. It was just after five and Will preferred to be cautious, allowing for the possibility of some caretaker or other being there late into the afternoon.

But the house was in darkness as he approached. He made his way to the side of the building, but as soon as he opened the door, he realised someone was inside. He could pick up the scent on the air and then, as he hesitated near the door, he heard a voice.

He walked slowly through the rooms, and as he neared the large room that now served as the gift shop, Will spotted a torch beam and realised there was only one person, and that he was talking and laughing to himself as he went about his business.

Will stood to the side of the door and looked into the room, ready to step back out of sight, and out of harm's way, if the torch beam moved in his direction. It was a boy of sixteen or seventeen, dressed in dark clothes, including a dark woollen hat pulled down far enough that only a little of his hair was visible from behind.

Will wondered how he'd got here, whether perhaps there was a bike left nearby, because he had to have come from one of the nearby villages, or from the outskirts of the city itself. A bike seemed most likely because as the boy looked through the items on display, he took only those small enough to fit into the bag he was carrying.

He was robbing the place, that had been immediately apparent. The cash till had been opened, the tray thrown aside on to the floor, though Will knew no money was left in there during the closed season. Now he was helping himself to various cheap souvenirs, perhaps unaware that the house contained many more valuable items.

The boy was mumbling to himself, laughing at some private joke. He reached a table laid out with various books for sale and tipped it over without looking at any of the volumes that fell to the floor in a small avalanche of pages. He moved to look at another display and the torch beam jumped towards the doorway. Will stood back against the wall, but his mind and body were racing against each other now, both heading towards the same conclusion.

His body told him that this was someone young and healthy, his blood carrying enough life force to last for months, even in these heightened times. Will's hunger intensified, the need feeling all the greater now that there was a potential way of feeding it.

His thoughts tumbled over each other too because this was a perfect victim. Yes, he probably had a family and would be missed in that sense, but what were the chances that he would have told anyone he was coming here to commit a crime? And if he had told anyone, wasn't it even less likely that they would reveal as much to the police?

Will could feed on this boy. He would be just one more of those many young people to walk out on an unprivileged life, to disappear without trace. People might search for him, but it was unlikely they would search for him here.

The boy headed to the door, but stopped as he got there and turned round to take one more look at the gift shop. Will took the opportunity to step out from the doorframe and stand behind him. The boy was looking at the wreckage, pleased with himself.

He produced one last little laugh at that private joke of his and turned directly into the path of Will's gaze. There was a moment of shock, of terror, as if he understood intuitively that this was about more than being discovered in the act of committing a crime, and then he was locked in and the torch dropped to the floor.

Will took the boy's gloved hands and lowered him until he was sitting on the floor, looking baffled, as if he couldn't think why he'd decided to sit down, only that he had. Will knelt down beside him, pulled off the gloves, pushed up the sleeves on the boy's top.

The boy looked down, as mesmerised as a spectator by his own murder, as Will took his small knife and drew a neat incision up the inside of his forearm.

Not a drop fell to the floor, Will locking his mouth on to the iron richness of the wound, greedily drinking in the warmth. The sense of nourishment was instant, the boy's life flooding in through his blood, filling the void at the centre of Will's own being.

As he moved to the other arm, he looked up at the boy's freckled face, his reddish-brown hair. He was still staring at his own arm in a state of mild confusion, slowly pulling his gaze away to look at Will. The boy's soul was still there, Will was certain of it, a presence behind the eyes that seemed untouched by the slow death of the body it inhabited. Will believed it to be so, and had to believe it to make his own existence bearable.

Once the boy was dead, Will pulled the sleeves down on his top to ensure no stray drops of blood fell when he moved the body. Then he took the boy's bag into the gift shop, replaced the items, straightened up the mess he'd made here and there.

Finally he toured the house. The only other thing he could see that was missing or moved was the sabre – he was certain he'd put it back, but in his starved and desperate state he'd perhaps left it in the tunnels or in the cellars. He searched for the point of entry too. There were no broken windows or locks, and no bike outside that he could see, but he found a door that was open, which was better still – it meant there was nothing to suggest anyone else had been in the house.

Once he was certain everything was secured, Will returned to the body. The brief sense of completion that came with feeding had already subsided, and now, as he looked at the boy's wide-eyed stare, he felt only a mild feeling of regret – no life, thought Will, could be so worthless as to be ended like this.

He picked up the torch and turned it off, putting it in the empty bag which he threw over his shoulder. He lifted the boy then, lighter than he'd expected, and carried him through to the library. He opened the first secret door, put the body on the floor and opened the wall to the steps.

He carried the body through the labyrinth to a point as far distant as he could find from the house, and laid it there, conscious that it would probably mummify rather than decompose in the air down there. He walked away, but turned and looked at the boy once more.

It was true he had been caught in an act of crime, something that throughout most of Will's long existence would have resulted in him being hanged and thrown into a common grave. But Will still felt he deserved more dignity than this, his body left in the open in a hidden tunnel.

The floor underneath was stone, and burying him in the parkland or woods above ran too much risk of the grave being found. Will went back to the house and down to the cellars, some of which were crammed with more materials than anyone would miss.

Over the next couple of hours he collected and transported three wooden crates, knocking all but two of the ends out of them, using the leftover wood to nail them together. He took a dust sheet, wrapped the body inside it, then placed it in the makeshift coffin.

Once that was done, he went to the large cellar that was used for storing unwanted furniture and ornaments. Each piece had a tag attached to it with a catalogue number, but Will doubted it was ever checked. On one of his previous wanderings he'd spotted a large crucifix for mounting on a wall and he took it back to the tunnels now, and placed it on top of the coffin.

He stood before the boy and thought for a moment, unsure whether he should say anything. He had seen funerals take place, but had never afforded any of his previous victims this courtesy. Nor had he actually attended a funeral since his own childhood.

In the end, Will offered one simple line of prayer, the only words he could think of that meant anything, that he hoped might one day be offered for him.

"Grant unto him eternal peace."

Will bowed his head, left the labyrinth and headed across the park. He felt stronger now, more firmly fixed to the world, but his spirits fell when he realised how long he'd been at the house. The evening was almost at an end and the Dangrave House common room looked deserted at first sight.

As Will reached his normal position he was able to see the only two people in that school who mattered to him in one way or another. Eloise was sitting on one of the sofas, reading a book. Nearby, Marcus Jenkins was playing chess, his opponent out of view beyond the frame of the window.

Eloise looked as beautiful as he'd ever seen her. She was reading, but looked distracted, and every now and then she glanced towards the window. She didn't look directly at him, just towards the window, in the general direction of where she knew Will usually stood.

The only thing Will didn't know was what she thought as she looked out, seeing only a reflection of the common room, but imagining the wintry park beyond.

Was she hoping for his return, worrying about him, or was she looking with dread in her heart, wishing he would disappear from her life as suddenly as he had walked into it two months before?

Whatever the answer, he doubted he would find out tonight. She closed the book and left the room, bidding goodnight to Marcus and the other boy. Will decided to wait for a while, but he knew somehow that she wouldn't come out, and not just because he had lied and said he wouldn't be back from the city until late.

As he stood there, he glanced up at the darkened window high above, realising that for the first time in many days, no one was observing him from up there. He didn't want to think of the obvious conclusion – he'd also told Chris that he wouldn't be back until late in the night, so perhaps word had got back to Wyndham's spies that they could take a night off from their duties.

His attention was drawn downwards again by movement in the common room. Marcus's opponent, his regular one, appeared as he prepared to leave. There seemed to be a brief discussion about putting the board away, but Marcus must have offered to do it because his friend left.

Marcus took his time placing the pieces back into the box, then putting the box and the board on a set of shelves on the far side of the common room. It looked for a moment as if he might simply leave then, but he stood for a moment, turned and looked directly at Will.

It unnerved Will no less than it had the first time he'd done it, and he took a step back before correcting himself. How Marcus always knew he was there was a mystery, but it was Marcus he'd come to see. Will walked forward until he was close enough to the window to be visible.

Again Marcus immediately understood the significance of Will appearing like that and put a hand up, telling Will to wait for a moment. Marcus left the room and Will retreated back into the shadows. A few minutes later, Marcus came out of the side door and walked towards Will with surprising speed.

Even before he'd reached Will, Marcus said, "What happened to Eloise?" His breath plumed out into the freezing air.

"What do people think happened to her?"

Marcus stopped a short distance from Will, momentarily deflected from his course by Will's question.

"No one thinks anything's happened to her. But it has, I can tell, and she didn't come out to see you tonight."

"She didn't think I'd be here – I returned early unexpectedly." He looked once more towards the room on the top floor, still unable to feel the watcher's eyes on him, which was probably all the better for Marcus. "You're right though. There are tunnels under the old abbey. We were searching them when Wyndham used his powers to move the walls around us. Eloise became trapped in a chamber, and before I could rescue her, Wyndham made her see things, horrific things."

Marcus didn't seem to doubt any of the events that had happened, but said, "How do you know it was Wyndham?"

"There are many factors pointing to him – I have no doubt about it."

Marcus nodded, thinking to himself, idly stroking his scar.

"Is it because I told him about you looking in the maze?"

"Perhaps."

"I need to be more careful about the things I tell him. Because I meant what I said about not hurting her – I won't."

"What about me?"

Marcus laughed and said, "You? What do you think I could do that'd hurt you?" He shivered. He'd come out in just the clothes he was wearing indoors and the cold was starting to eat its way through him.

"You should go inside," said Will. "But I wanted to ask you, and I understand if your loyalty prevents you from answering, did you ever visit Wyndham's house?"

Marcus took a moment, then said, "No, I can tell you that. I did, but it was night-time and the car he took me in had blacked-out windows. He took me in the same car when he brought me here and that time the windows were just tinted, so it must be something he does."

"So you don't know where the house is?"

Marcus paused, thinking the question over before responding.

"I don't believe you're everything he's said about you, I don't even know if I believe any of it, but it's true what you said about loyalty. And like I said, he's paying my way. You can't expect me to . . ."

"No, I don't, and I quite understand. I hope only that you'll change your mind at some point. For now I'll bid you goodnight."

Marcus nodded again as if acknowledging that Will had backed down on a point of principle. He walked away, but stopped after a few paces and said, "I'll tell you one thing about him though. He grew up around here somewhere, but it wasn't recent."

"What makes you say that?"

"When we came here the first time, he said to me he knew this house when he was young. I asked if he went to school here. He was kind of daydreaming, you know, and he said no, it hadn't been a school then, but he'd known the family that lived here. Well, it's been a school for over a hundred and fifty years." Marcus gave a little laugh, taking some pleasure in being able to share his deductions with someone. "So either Mr Wyndham's not all there in the head, or he's got more in common with you than you realise."

He raised his hand in a wave, just as he'd done that night by the river, then turned and walked back into the school. Will watched him go, intrigued and confused by the things Marcus had told him. How could Wyndham be so old if he was a normal living human, and how could it be that he had known the Dangraves?

Most of all, he wondered, if he and Wyndham had so much shared history in this city and its surrounds, was it possible that they had encountered each other before? Could that be the real key to Wyndham's determination to destroy him?

21

My journey home took longer and was more troublesome than I would have liked, and it was early in the year 1800 when I finally reached the city. I took rooms in an inn on the first night, given that I arrived late and that the city was shrouded in fog.

Beyond that, I had thought to return home, but as I lay in bed that first night, I came to think that I no longer had a home. Though I had grown up there, I had failed to grow old. I had become a stranger this last half-century, and not only because of my continued absence.

The next afternoon, with the fog still hanging densely over a frozen landscape, I had my coachman take me the five miles or so to the home of my childhood. And when I reached the house and asked for Lord Bowcastle, I didn't even know if I would be met by my brother or by his son, such had been the lack of communication between us in recent years.

When asked who was calling, I told the servant it was a distant cousin, and was then taken through to the library where I found my brother, now seventy-five years old, sitting in front of the fire with a book resting on his lap. I was invited to sit, drinks were poured, we were left alone.

He smiled at me, in some confusion, and said, "Phillip Wyndham, Peckham said, so you must be a cousin through the line of my father's younger brothers, but I thought . . ."

I could have wept for he was still quite recognisably my brother, the brother who'd always been so much stronger than I, so much bigger too for most of our shared history, yet he was so frail now, an old man in decline. Only his eyes retained their youthful vigour but that only made it all the more upsetting.

"Tom, it's me, Phillip. I am not your cousin, I am your brother."

He smiled and said, "You look very much like him. You're his son?"

"No, I am your brother, returned from my travels at last."

"But you haven't changed at all." He was hopeful for a moment, then suspicious as he said, "You're a charlatan, sir, if you say that. You cannot be my brother – he would be a man of sixty-six now. You look less than forty."

"My journey wasn't in vain, Tom. I have learned

things I never dreamt of learning, and not least amongst them was this, the ability to hold back time." I could see that he still struggled to believe me, so I said, "You have a scar on the outside of your left forearm where one of our dogs bit you – a pointer. I was six, you were fifteen. Our father wanted to beat the dog, but you said it was you who should be beaten for you'd antagonised the poor animal. He laughed and said then let that be a lesson in itself. Why do I remember this when I was so young? Because it was I who antagonised the dog that day, because you incurred the bite in trying to separate us. Our father was a kind man, I don't think he ever beat either of us, but you took the blame for me all the same."

My brother's eyes glistened with tears as he said, "But how can this be?"

I explained the events of the last half-century as best I could and then we reminisced for a little while, and he told me of the deaths of our parents. And as darkness was falling, he said, "Is it too late for me, to learn what you know?"

"It is, Tom," I said.

"I know it, yet I would give you my title and all I possess in exchange for your knowledge."

I believed him, but even if it had been within my power to share what I knew, it takes a certain type of person to make the sacrifices required of this existence.

I visited him again many times over the remaining five years of his life, but I insisted on never meeting Lady Bowcastle, and after his death, I never returned there again, even though I have passed the estate many times and know my brother's descendants to live there still.

The property in which my mother had grown up now belonged to me and I considered moving in there, thinking it might provide a link to the demon, but I knew it would not be appropriate for my very specific needs. Instead I bought a large mansion house set in its own parkland a little outside the city and it is there that I've remained ever since.

Of course, living anywhere in this country has become increasingly difficult in a world of bureaucracy, of forms and regulations. The Breakstorm Trust and others like it have enabled me to live below the radar, but it has not always been easy. At least in those early days my life was reasonably unhindered by such things.

Over the following years I sifted the city's records, studied the daily papers for unusual murders across the country, and visited every corner of these islands little by little. I encountered vampires, killed them where I could, learned about them. The records offered hints of the vampire activity I knew to expect in this city, but there had been nothing recent, and nothing to suggest the presence of the demon I sought – at this stage I still didn't even know his name, only that my mother had called him Will-o'-the-wisp.

The first real sign came in the winter of 1812. A woman was murdered near the cathedral, torn at the neck as if by some wild animal, the blood drained from her. She was a common prostitute and the authorities made little effort to find the killer, but when I investigated, I found news that was both promising and disappointing.

It was soon clear that this wasn't the work of the demon I was looking for, but from the wounds inflicted on the body, I knew a vampire to be responsible. Eyewitnesses described an enormous man dressed in ancient clothes, wearing his hair long, suggesting in his appearance something of a Viking warrior. Not my demon then, but I had to believe there was some connection between the two.

In the following year, another death occurred that aroused my attention. A boy of fourteen had been found dead in the stable of a coaching inn. In an attempt, perhaps, to protect his reputation and allow him a proper burial, it was speculated that he had torn his arm on a nail protruding from an upright timber next to where the body was found, that he'd fainted and bled to death.

There was indeed blood on the nail, but the nature of the wound to the boy's arm might have led the more determined observer to conclude that it couldn't have been inflicted by accident, that the boy had intended to kill himself, a crime at the time, one that would have brought shame on his family and seen him buried in unconsecrated ground.

One of my servants alerted me to the news very quickly and I arrived at the stable whilst the body was still in situ. It was a pitiful sight. He was a slim, dark-haired boy, small for his age, the makings of a handsome face. He'd been a stable boy, but had – imagine my horror at hearing it – ridden two winners for Lord Bowcastle (my nephew) at the recent horse races.

One of his shirt sleeves was rolled up above the site of the wound, but I knew instantly that this was neither an accident nor suicide. The cut was too clean to have been inflicted by the nail, though the blood on the nail suggested someone had been keen for it to be seen that way. More importantly, though he had died through loss of blood, there was hardly any on the straw upon which he lay.

The boy had been murdered, and though I couldn't be sure, my instinct told me that the demon had emerged once more into the city, that this was his work. It appeared he had chosen to use a knife rather than the animal savagery I'd witnessed so many times before, but that in itself spoke of the evil intelligence that had so unsettled my mother.

George Cuthbertson. Perhaps it matters not at all to William of Mercia, but that was the name of the fourteen-year-old boy he murdered that night, whose future he snuffed out with as little thought as one might blow out a candle.

Think about George Cuthbertson for a moment, about the life he might have led, the sweetheart he might have married, the children and grandchildren, the descendants living to this day who would have traced their family tree and found him, a talented horseman, winner of racing trophies. That life and all those other lives were stolen because William of Mercia believed he was more deserving of George Cuthbertson's life force than the boy himself.

I visited George's family afterwards, his widowed mother, his three younger brothers and two younger sisters, all reliant to some extent on George's financial contribution. Their devastation was heart-rending.

I did what I could, helping them financially, paying for an education for the children. And it brings some comfort that all three brothers made decent careers, one becoming an engineer, another a teacher, that the two sisters both married well. All long dead now of course, *and they never knew the biggest part of what I did for them because I preferred to hide my kindness behind one of the many trusts I'd established.*

More importantly, for the first time ever, George Cuthbertson's death helped me fully understand that this was not just a personal crusade. I had a public duty to rid the world of such an evil as the demon I would one day learn to call William of Mercia. At that point in time I thought him only another vampire, but as wicked as all those other demons were, I was yet to appreciate that his evil was of another dimension entirely.

22

Will was about to leave the house, unsure whether Eloise would want to see him, when he saw her walking across the lawns towards him. It had started to snow at last and large heavy flakes fell around her, settling on her coat and in her hair.

He waited with the door open, like someone inviting her into his own home. She slowed as she saw him and offered a subdued smile that might have been an apology or at least a peace offering. She gave him a brief hug, but it felt like a formality rather than the tentative intimacies he'd become familiar with.

"I'm glad you came," said Will.

"You're not angry with me?"

"Why would I be angry? Something very disturbing happened to you."

"I know, but it wasn't you, it was Wyndham, and I'm angry with myself that he made me suspect you or look at you differently."

It was ridiculous, but Will felt himself hurt by her

admission. He'd thought as much this last day or so, but for her to say it aloud, that her faith in him had been shaken, wounded him deeply.

He said only, "We'll both face similar tests before this is over." Then, as an afterthought, he said, "And if you ever decide you want no further part in this, I would think no less of you."

Eloise looked alarmed. "No, absolutely not – I *am* part of this, whether I like it or not."

"Then we'll say no more about it."

He turned to close the door, but looked out through the falling snow, wondering if she'd been followed from the school. He couldn't see anyone, but then he doubted she would need to be followed closely – there were only so many places she might be heading on foot.

Eloise followed his gaze, but misunderstood its purpose and said, "It's beautiful, isn't it? I love the snow."

Will smiled. He'd always loved it too, because after a heavy snowfall, the city looked little different from the city he'd known as a boy. Deep snow had that gift for him, not only of stopping time, but of erasing it. Sometimes it was easy to believe that the thaw would reveal the place just as he'd once known it.

He closed the door and said, "Where should we go?"

"The library," she said, as if it was obvious.

It had become their most regular room because it had

no large windows, which meant it was safer having a lamp on in there. Will thought she might have wanted to avoid it now, given its proximity to the tunnels, but Eloise had sounded determined.

He led her through as he had so many times before and turned on two of the lamps. Eloise turned one of them back off and sat on one of the deep leather sofas. Will sat on the sofa opposite, a large table between them which might once have been laden with books.

"So, what's the plan?"

Her tone was businesslike, but Will said, "I have little idea. I've tried to find out where Wyndham lives, but with no success so far. I don't even know why I'm trying to find that out – perhaps only because I have so little notion of what I should do next."

"The gateway, it's gone?"

"Presumably it's still there, but it's impossible to get anywhere close to it using the tunnels. There could be another way in, but I don't know how we'd even begin to find it."

Eloise looked around the room at the books and said, "If there's another way in, Henry would have known about it, so his library might contain a clue."

Will smiled. "But this isn't Henry's library – that's in the city and as you know, I'm familiar with most of the works there." Even as he said it, he realised that he'd never read the section in Henry's Doomsday Book that related to Marland. But he didn't have the chance to share that thought.

Eloise suddenly said, "Oh my God! I was just thinking how well you looked now, and then I realised. You've fed!" Her tone was disturbingly accusatory. "That's why you stayed in the city, why you came back late last night."

Oddly, Will had a sudden memory of the adult Arabella Harriman stepping down from her carriage all those years ago, the casual stare, the recollection of his face, the horror, the light fading in her eyes as she faltered. It was how all his relationships with the living had to end.

"I stayed in the city because . . . I could tell you were uncomfortable being around me and I did not want to see you so. I had no thought of feeding, and as it happens, I came back here early yesterday evening and accidentally interrupted a burglary."

"A burglary? One person or . . ."

"One."

"So you killed him."

"I fed. And yes, I killed him." She was falling away from him again, but it was Will who felt amazed now, saying, "You have known what I am since the beginning. I have repeatedly told you what you know to be true, that I am a monster, that I was once a good person, but that my very existence is wicked. And you saw what has been happening to me these last days – did you think I could continue without blood indefinitely?"

"Of course I didn't!" Eloise jumped up and paced up and down in front of the sofa. "But you can't expect me just to accept it! You murdered someone. You've murdered a lot of people."

"Does a hawk murder a sparrow? I kill out of necessity, not for amusement. And I accept that it's difficult for you – in the early days it was difficult for me."

Those words calmed her a little, as if they gave him back a touch of humanity. She sat down again.

"But yes, I did kill yesterday, and you need to know that I will kill again unless I am killed first or unless my destiny allows me to escape the shackles of my sickness." He saw a flicker of uneasiness pass over her eyes and added quickly, "And what you saw was not my destiny, only what Wyndham would wish you to believe."

"I know." She thought for a second and said, "What did you do with the body?"

"I laid it to rest in the tunnels. I couldn't bury it, but I wrapped it in a shroud and made a coffin of sorts." She looked intrigued, as if she'd learned something new about him, but he intercepted her question, saying, "No, it isn't what I usually do. I buried someone some seven hundred years ago, but . . . she was different. I interred the boy last night and I'm not sure why, except that seeing the spirits of my past victims affected me in some way."

Eloise didn't respond directly, but hit upon one word and said, "Boy? He was young?"

"Perhaps your age or a little older." Will decided against mentioning the advantage of that, the amount of life force that had been in his blood.

"What did he look like?"

The question was simply put, but her tone suggested she wanted to know for a specific reason.

"A little taller than me, reddish-brown hair, brown eyes. Pale but with a freckly complexion."

Eloise started to shake her head as he spoke, then said, "This can't be happening. Are you sure he was a burglar?"

"He was in the process of helping himself to various items from the shop, and had broken into the cash register. I'm certain he was a burglar. Why do you ask?"

"Because a sixth-former called Alex Shawcross has disappeared from the school. Everyone's mystified because he doesn't seem to have taken anything with him and he's a star pupil – academic, sporty. You just described him."

"Is he wealthy?"

She nodded. "That's one of the reasons it's caused

such a fuss – his family owns a big chunk of Scotland and his dad's the chairman of some huge multinational conglomerate."

"But personally?"

"Oh, he's got plenty of cash, one of those guys who's always got all the latest gadgets, you know the type." Will smiled a little because she'd forgotten for a moment that he *didn't* know that or any other type. "Why do you ask?"

"Because I doubt it can be the same person, despite the similarity. The person you describe doesn't need money, and doesn't sound like the kind of person who would break into a house and its gift shop for the thrill of it alone."

He was troubled though by the memory of not finding a bike. His victim had come on foot which suggested that he had not come far.

Eloise said quite abruptly, "There's only one way to be sure – show me."

"What difference will it make? Either way a boy will be missing and we will know he's dead. Either way he is unlikely to be traced here."

"True, but it would give me peace of mind."

"It will give you peace of mind to know that the boy I killed is poor rather than one of your privileged schoolfellows? I find that odd indeed, because I can

216

assure you the poverty of my victims gives me no great peace of mind."

She looked wrong-footed by his comment and said, "I didn't mean it like that. I just need to know."

Will stood and said, "As you wish. It will mean going back into the labyrinth."

Eloise stood too, by way of an answer, though Will thought he detected a slight apprehension creeping into her eyes. He led the way and when they reached the top of the steps, he looked at her.

"Wyndham appears to constantly move from one type of attack to another, so I doubt he'll set about us again down there, but I want you to know, I won't let anything happen to you."

"You did last time." Even before he could respond, she looked mortified and said, "I'm sorry, I didn't mean that. I know you got me out of there."

He laughed it off and said, "So I'm only human after all."

She smiled too, but he couldn't help but feel the underlying tension that had caused her to speak like that. The last time they'd stood on these steps together he had kissed her, the briefest moment of pleasure, and now it felt as far away from him as those sunny afternoons he dreamt of.

They walked the first part in silence, but once they

entered the tunnels proper, Eloise started to talk, all nervous energy as she said, "It's a shame that all of this is hidden, and ruined now I suppose, the way it's all been moved around. It'd be like a World Heritage Site or something if they did find it. Overrun with tourists – can you imagine?"

She wasn't looking for much of a response from Will, and he allowed her to talk on, imagining she was doing her best not to think about what had happened to her down here. Perhaps she was also trying not to think about what they were doing here now.

When Will turned into the long tunnel where he'd laid the boy to rest, he saw his efforts with fresh eyes. He'd done his best under the circumstances, but any dignity he thought he'd given the boy in death melted away when he saw the ramshackle wooden coffin. Only the crucifix that lay on top of it hinted at the respect he'd hoped to show.

Eloise stopped a little way short.

"Are you sure you want to go through with this?"

She nodded and stepped closer. Will took the crucifix and placed it carefully on the floor. He pulled open the lid of the crate that covered the boy's head and chest, and slowly pulled the shroud free without yet exposing the face. He lifted it enough to see the features himself – they had sunken a little, but he'd been right about the

218

air down here, the dryness and the cold having left the boy almost as he'd been just after death.

Will looked up at Eloise and she said, "I'm ready."

He pulled the shroud back and she took a step closer then stopped abruptly, confused for a moment, then nodded as she stepped backwards, bumping into the wall behind her and reaching a hand out to steady herself.

Will wrapped the shroud round the boy again, then replaced the lid and the crucifix. Once he'd done that, he stood and said, "Is it him?"

"It's him." She looked at Will and said, "What are we going to do? They're looking for him."

"We're not going to do anything. His body will remain at peace here."

"But his family – they'll want to know what happened to him."

"True." Will thought about it and said, "There's a fast-running brook not far from here. I could place the body in the water, together with a knife, an apparent suicide. The water would explain why there was no blood. I'm not certain how much more comforting that would be to his family than simply not knowing his fate."

Eloise looked aghast as she said, "You're serious? You think that's a solution, dumping his body in a stream, making his family think he killed himself?"

"No, there is no solution. I can't bring him back to life. I've done the best I can for him in death." He looked again at the coffin, meagre, but more than he'd done for his other victims. "I have to ask again, would you have been so concerned about his family's pain if it had not been Alex Shawcross in that box?"

"Of course I would! It's just that I knew him."

"Did you like him?"

"He was OK – I mean, I didn't know him that well, but he was OK. He didn't deserve this."

"Nobody does," said Will. "But what intrigues me is what he was doing here, breaking into this house."

"I don't know, Will, doing something stupid. People do stupid things sometimes, like breaking into places for the hell of it, like running away from school to live rough in the city."

She gave him an exasperated look and turned and walked away. He followed her, making sure she didn't take a wrong turn, but in her irritation and upset she somehow managed to remember the route without even thinking about it.

And as he walked, Will thought over the night before, finding the boy he now knew to be Alex Shawcross, the way he'd laughed and talked to himself, the way he'd gone to the specific trouble of messing the place up. It came to him at once.

Alex Shawcross had been there on Wyndham's business, staging a break-in to ensure that the house would have been searched from top to bottom, making it just a little bit harder for Will to stay there. The only question was why Wyndham would have sent him late in the afternoon when it was dark, knowing the danger for the boy, unless word had got to Wyndham that Will wouldn't be returning until late in the evening. That was something only Chris or Rachel could have told him.

There could be another reason, and Will had to accept that it might have been just as Eloise had said, that this otherwise exemplary boy had decided to break into a country house in a reckless moment. But Will thought back again to him tipping over that table of books and was certain he was right.

He waited till they reached the library again and said, "Eloise, is it possible the boy was here on Wyndham's business?"

"Alex," said Eloise. "The boy had a name and it was Alex, and why would Wyndham want him to break into a house?"

"Because he knows I'm staying here, because a burglary would have resulted in police searching the house, just one more thing to make it difficult for me to remain here."

"But if Wyndham knows you live here, why would

he send Alex – and I know you see Wyndham's spies everywhere, but I really doubt Alex Shawcross would have been one of them – but why would he send Alex here after dark, knowing what could happen to him?"

"Perhaps he'd heard that I wasn't going to be back until late last night."

"I'm the only person who knew that, and . . ." She rolled her eyes and said, "Oh, here we go again, Chris and Rachel! Even now, after everything they've done for us, you still can't get it out of your head . . ."

"Only a few days ago it was you who didn't trust Chris."

"You're twisting what I said. And they've been so kind. Why would they do that if they were working for him?"

Will could see the conversation was going nowhere, and perhaps they didn't even need to know now why Alex Shawcross had been here. If he had been working for Wyndham, the plan had been thwarted. They'd be better served preparing for Wyndham's next assault, not dissecting the last.

"Well, it doesn't matter now."

Eloise was apparently determined to quarrel and threw her arms in the air. "Of course it matters. Alex is dead. And you think the two people who've helped us the most are with Wyndham. Of course that matters."

Will was about to respond, though he was struggling to think what words might calm her, when he stopped, suddenly conscious that they were not alone. He breathed in deeply and looked at her and spoke quietly.

"There's someone in the house."

She looked ready to reply with another outburst, but caught herself and whispered, "What should we do?"

Before Will could answer, they heard a child's laugh. They turned, looking towards the door. No one was there, but then the laugh came again, and hurried footsteps, and a little girl ran into the library. She was dressed for another age, and as she ran through the library, her pale blue dress rustled and she continued to laugh to herself. She didn't notice Will and Eloise, but it was as if she failed to notice them in her own excitement rather than because she was a spirit. She looked and sounded quite real.

Eloise stared open-mouthed as the girl ran the length of the room and then hid behind a large leather armchair.

"Is that who you could . . ."

Will shook his head, taking in the air, still picking up a human scent, but he put his finger to his lips and looked towards the armchair. They could still hear the little girl laughing quietly in her hiding place.

"A ghost," said Will.

Eloise looked at the chair that concealed her and whispered, "But she looked real."

Will also kept his voice low, saying, "There is someone else living in this house, but not her. And if she is not living, what else could she be?"

Another laugh emerged from where the child hid. Will started to move towards the armchair and Eloise joined him. It was a little girl, nothing more, and yet both of them walked tentatively, a little nervous of what they might find there.

23

They both walked to the side of the armchair and looked down. There was the little girl, curled up into a ball with her face obscured, still laughing, her blonde ringlets tied in ribbons the same colour as her dress.

As if realising that they were standing there, she looked up, saw them and screamed. Eloise jumped backwards at the noise, but Will realised immediately that it wasn't a scream of terror, but of being found about her hide-and-seek.

The girl laughed immediately afterwards, jumped up and ran off, doing a full circuit of the library before she left through the door where she'd entered. Still, Will could detect another human scent from somewhere in the house, but there were indistinct noises everywhere, like a house creaking and groaning on a stormy night.

"How weird was . . ." said Eloise, but stopped as footsteps emerged from within the far wall. A moment later, the door to the secret passage opened and a man of advancing years appeared, portly, wearing a heavy brocade dressing gown. He crossed the library, ran his finger along one of the shelves, selected a book and disappeared as he'd come.

They listened to his footsteps retreating and then heard the unmistakable sound of a billiard ball being struck, hitting another. Eloise didn't hesitate, but headed out towards the billiard room. Will followed her, ready to lead her through the darkness, but there was no need – the rest of the house was lit in some way, as if the air itself was luminous.

They crossed the hall, stopping only as a maid rushed in from the main door and up the stairs in front of them. The reception rooms on this wing of the house were interconnected and before they entered the dining room, Will stopped Eloise.

He whispered, "Stay behind me. These may be ghosts, but there is a living person here too."

"Wyndham?"

"I don't know." He hoped so, and yet he knew Wyndham wouldn't show himself unless he was confident of being stronger than Will. It was the only reason, Will was certain, that the sorcerer had not shown himself yet.

They moved through the dining room and drawing room, but the connecting doors were all open and they could already see two young men about a game of billiards in the room beyond. As Will and Eloise got closer, they put down their cues and left through the door into the next room, out of sight.

Will and Eloise stepped inside the billiard room, looking at the table and the unfinished game. Will looked briefly at the wall, the two sabres reminding him that he had left the third somewhere. He still had a clear memory of replacing it, but he had done so more than once, so perhaps his memory tricked him now.

Suddenly a woman's voice called out behind them, "Really, Mr Wetherton, I think you tease us!" As Will and Eloise turned, a party of people laughed, joining in with the lady's accusation, with one man, presumably Wetherton, making a light-hearted attempt to defend himself.

They were in the dining room, a full dinner apparent in the misty light that filled the house, servants in attendance, the gentle clatter of silverware on china. Will and Eloise started to walk back across the drawing room towards them, but stopped midway as the spirits all stood as one and moved towards the far doors, almost as if responding to Will and Eloise's approach.

It seemed there was no need to whisper now, but Eloise still spoke quietly as she said, "What's going on? It's as if they know we're here."

Will shook his head, the only answer he could give, and continued towards the doors that divided drawing and dining rooms. The rest of the dinner guests were filing out of the door beyond, the last being the young lady who'd made the humorous accusation.

She was almost through the door, ready to close it behind her, when she looked back and stared directly at Will. It was a look tinged with sadness and concern, so full of misgiving that Will felt uneasy in response. It was as if she was trying to tell him something or warn him, but of what?

The far door closed, but the house was still full of noise. He heard footsteps running overhead, more giggling, though not the same child – this was a boy, he thought. Two billiard balls cracked together, but when Will and Eloise turned, no one was there behind them. Will stared for a second as the two balls rolled about the table and slowly came to rest.

A door slammed, then another, then every door on the floor above them shut one after the other, sounding like a volley of gunshots. It had seemed a harmless display until now, but in some subtle way the atmosphere had suddenly become sinister.

Eloise looked at him, all their previous disagreements forgotten as she said, "What should we do?"

Will didn't need to answer. The air around them

appeared to crackle, sparks of static here and there around the room which flew together as if drawn by a magnetic force, quickly forming into something resembling human shapes.

A harsh whisper close to them said, "Go!"

They turned, moving into the middle of the room, as the figures became clearer. It was the seven witches, but looking less solid than previously, as if they were struggling to form themselves.

Will said, "Is this your work?"

The one who spoke was standing near the entrance to the billiard room, but though the witches were all visible now, Will could still see through her to the table beyond.

Her voice was urgent, almost panicked, as she said, "Go! Get out of this house. Get out of this house now!"

The air crackled around them, and as if in fear themselves, the spirits appeared to catapult away, disappearing through the walls. A door slammed somewhere nearby. More noises sounded, of things moving throughout the house.

Will turned to Eloise, about to tell her to run, when he noticed her breath rising as mist in the cold. A sliding noise sounded all around them and every picture in the room crashed to the floor. The doors to the dining room slammed shut.

"Will?"

He reached out and took her hand, then heard an ominous clattering noise from the billiard room. He saw, almost too late, one of the sabres spinning through the air towards them, towards Eloise. He leapt forward and caught it by the blade in his right hand, immediately taking hold of the hilt with his left, ready to use it, for all a sabre might do against such forces.

The house was clattering with noise and disturbance. The tables and chairs around them were rattling on the floor. And then there was that human scent, growing stronger now, getting closer.

"Someone's coming," said Will, looking to the billiard room.

And then he was there, standing in the open doorway between the two rooms, looking amazed, but as disturbingly calm as ever. Marcus Jenkins.

He laughed and said, "What's going on?"

Eloise pointed and said, "What are you doing here?"

Marcus was still smiling, still apparently unconcerned as he started walking towards them and said, "Duh? Following you."

He heard a noise behind him and his eyes betrayed a hundred calculations taking place at once: the sound he'd heard, the sabre in Will's hand, his position between the two of them and the billiard room.

He moved incredibly quickly, grabbing a chair,

spinning round as he held it up to intercept the other sabre, which embedded itself in the chair back. He grabbed the hilt of the sword and pulled it free, throwing the chair to the floor and standing ready.

Will doubted Marcus had ever handled a sword before and yet he stood with the poise of someone who'd seen combat many times. He still wasn't quick enough to spot one of the billiard balls as it shot past him, and turned only as it flew towards Eloise's head.

Will was quicker, responding instinctively and slicing the ball in half with an explosive crack.

For the first time, Marcus appeared shocked as he looked at Eloise and shouted over the increasing noise, "That was aiming for your head."

"Now you believe me," said Will. "This is Wyndham's work – he can't kill me so he's trying to kill Eloise. We have to get out of here."

There was more noise from the billiard room and Marcus turned and fought to pull the doors shut, shouting, "Go! I'll hold the doors till you're out."

Will moved towards the dining room doors, but immediately both those doors and the others being held by Marcus started to be bombarded with objects that thundered against the wood and fell to the floor. Once more, the objects in the room about them started to move too. A picture suddenly flew from the floor across the room, Will knocking it down before it reached Eloise.

He picked up the chair Marcus had used and threw it hard at the window with such force that the glass and the entire frame shattered and exploded outwards on to the snow-covered gardens. Eloise didn't need to be told what to do – she ran and jumped over the low sill and kept running until she was far enough to turn and look back.

Will looked at Marcus and said, "Come on."

"You first!"

Will jumped out through the window and a few moments later, Marcus followed with the sound of the billiard room doors bursting open behind him and slamming against the walls. He reached Will and Eloise and immediately turned and held the sabre out in front of him, preparing to defend against whatever attack might follow them.

Nothing else left the house though. As the three of them stood there in the falling snow, Will and Marcus flanking Eloise, the house almost instantly became quiet. Then a calmer, more methodical noise started to emerge from the various rooms.

Marcus looked puzzled. "What now?"

Eloise said, "It sounds . . . it sounds like someone tidying up."

She let out a small scream then as the chair that

Will had used to break the window flew back into the drawing room as if pulled on an elastic cord. A moment later, the shattered glass and the wooden frame did the same, flying away from the ground and reforming unbroken where they had been before.

Indistinct shadows still moved about beyond the lit windows, but as the sounds slowly faded, so did the human forms, the spirit world retreating again, leaving the house as it had been a little while before. Apart from the two sabres, Will could imagine not a single thing would be out of place in there. And again, if it hadn't been for his intentions, Will would have admired Wyndham for being able to perform such sorcery.

The lights started to dim. All the shadows had disappeared, but just as it seemed the spirits were gone, a silhouette appeared in one of the upstairs rooms, a female figure who stood as if looking down at them. It was a shadow, nothing more, but Will was certain it was the young lady they'd seen at dinner, the lady who'd looked back at him with such concern.

"What's up, Will?" He turned to look at Eloise, smiling reassurance, and when he looked back, the window was empty and the light that had filled the house faded abruptly. "Nothing. I was just thinking how odd it was, those spirits we just saw, the little girl and the man with the book, the young men playing billiards, the party at dinner, they were . . . nothing, I was just thinking, that's all."

Marcus turned to look at the two of them, intrigued now that he was able to watch them closely.

Eloise appeared unaware of his gaze and instead looked at Will, the tenderness back in her expression as she said, "You were thinking that they were your family, not your own descendants perhaps, but still your family."

"Yes, that's what I was thinking." He looked at Marcus who was idly stroking his scar. "I want to thank you for what you did in there."

Marcus shrugged and Eloise said, "I'm sorry. Of course – Marcus, thank you. That sabre was flying towards me, without a doubt."

"You're welcome, but Will would've stopped it. Who knows, maybe one day I'll save you properly." He laughed at the thought.

Will said, "What will you tell Wyndham?"

Marcus shook his head. "Nothing, not any more. Maybe I'll write in the book to keep him sweet for a while, but I don't like what he's doing, hurting a girl and all that, it doesn't seem right." He turned to Eloise. "And I know I was with Taz and them that night down by the river, but I didn't know what I was doing, not until I saw Will. It's weird, I had a sort of . . ."

234

He struggled to find a suitable word, and Eloise said, "An epiphany."

"Is that what you call it? I like that – an epiphany." He smiled. "And I suppose I knew then that it'd come to this sooner or later – I'm on your side now. If you'll trust me."

Eloise looked wary, but Will didn't hesitate. "You're a welcome ally. Though I have little idea what we can do, or where we can even go that will be safe for Eloise."

"The school chapel," said Marcus as if stating the obvious. "He has no powers in the chapel. He told me that."

Will said, "You must be mistaken – he's attacked me in a church before now."

Marcus shook his head. "No, I don't mean churches in general, just the school chapel."

Eloise looked uncertain again, fearing a trap, and said, "Will . . ."

But Marcus appeared to read her thoughts and said, "It's natural for you not to trust me, but what can I do? I give you my word, that's all, that the chapel's where we'll be safe."

Will and Eloise exchanged glances, enough to agree with each other, and without saying anything else, they started walking back towards the school, three figures lost together in a snowy landscape. Whether or not they were right to trust Marcus, Will couldn't help but see the symbolism, that here he was again, seeking sanctuary from the dangers of the world in a place that was holy.

24

By the time they reached the school they were covered with snow. It was not yet in total darkness and they stopped for a moment in Will's usual position and looked at the few remaining people in the common room. Marcus's usual chess partner was reading a book.

Will looked up at the darkened window on the top floor, but for the second night running he could tell that no one was there. Briefly he wondered if the watcher had been Alex Shawcross, if that was why he'd been absent these last two nights.

Perhaps Eloise would have felt differently about him if she'd realised the boy might have been the one who'd drawn the chalk diagram beneath her bed, who'd played a part in trying to kill her. But Will said nothing, not wanting to raise any subject that might remind her of the negative emotions they'd so recently left behind.

Eloise said, "Which is the best door, do you think, if we want to get to the chapel without being seen?"

Her question was addressed to Marcus. It was a nice

touch, thought Will, given that she knew the school a lot better than the new boy – it suggested a desire to include him, which in turn suggested she now accepted him.

Marcus turned to Will and said, "Can you open any door?"

"Yes."

He turned back to Eloise and said, "The door to the kitchens. There's a back corridor from there that takes us close to the steps down to the chapel."

Eloise looked at Will, smiling as she said, "He's right. Round the back."

They walked the long way around rather than pass the front of the school, walking past one of the other common rooms which Eloise and Marcus looked at with mild contempt, though to Will it looked much the same as their own.

They also passed Dr Higson's office. Despite the late hour, he was still in there, reading through paperwork at his desk.

Marcus said, "Have you seen Dr Higson? He's sprained his wrist or something, got his hand all bandaged up."

"How?"

"Fell on his morning run."

"Poor him," said Eloise and turned to Will. "That's the headmaster in there. He's such a sweet man – when I came back after Christmas, he couldn't have been nicer about it really. Didn't lecture me about running away or living rough, just asked if I needed any help catching up. So cool."

Will nodded, staring in like a visitor being shown the sights. Clearly Chris and Rachel had forgotten to tell Eloise that Will would be speaking with Higson about her more recent absence – perhaps she thought they'd made her excuses for her. It was equally clear that neither Eloise nor Marcus suspected Higson or thought there might be another explanation for his injury.

The kitchens were empty and they moved through them quickly, into the wood-panelled back corridor and out through another door, which itself was designed to look like a panelled wall from the other side. They turned right and down the steps into the short corridor that led to the chapel.

Once inside with the door closed, Eloise turned on one of the lights and said, "Don't worry, we won't be heard in here – you can't hear a thing from the other side of that door."

Will nodded and walked up the aisle, struck by how large it was for a family chapel, if not for the school that now used it. Had it been an act of guilt perhaps, built to make amends for having gained so much from the destruction of Marland Abbey itself?

It was charming in its own way, but very much of its age, full of fine artwork. It didn't come close to the simple, monumental beauty of Will's church, a building which he sometimes thought looked as if it had sprung out of the rock fully formed, a natural wonder rather than a man-made one. But this chapel was beautiful nonetheless.

He noted the steps leading down to a gate and a crypt beyond. He could explore it in due course, and if it proved unsafe to return to the new house for a time, he could quite possibly stay here. If what Marcus had said about Wyndham's powers failing in this chapel was true, it could be the perfect lair for Will.

That in itself raised a question though. This was just a family chapel, built by his brother's descendants, so why could Wyndham not work his magic here. He had managed to attack Will in the heart of the city cathedral, in his own chambers deep beneath it, so why should this holy place prove a barrier to him?

Marcus had sat down on the front pew, placing the sabre next to him, but Will walked over to him and said, "Did Wyndham tell you why his powers don't work in here?"

"He doesn't know. He told me to avoid confronting you in here – not that he told me to confront you at all – because his powers didn't reach here and he wouldn't be able to protect me."

Eloise came and sat on the altar step facing Marcus. "Has he protected you elsewhere?"

"Not that I know of – he didn't do much tonight, did he?"

Will said, "About the chapel?"

Marcus nodded. "I asked him, is it because it's a church, and he got a bit funny with me, said why would a church stop the powers of good from destroying evil? Then he calmed down and said he didn't know why this particular chapel was a problem for him. It just is."

Will smiled, thinking how he'd misdirected Chris by pretending the chapel was significant, and now it seemed it really was. He looked up at the roof and around the walls, and said to himself as much as to them, "I suspect Henry would know, if only he was here to share his secret."

Marcus followed Will's gaze and said, "Who's Henry?"

"The man who built it," said Eloise. "What do you know about Wyndham?"

"Not much. He's old. What I mean to say is, he looks about fifty, I'd say, grey hair, always wearing a suit. But he's *old*. I think he's at least two hundred, but probably more."

"How can you be so certain?"

Will answered for him. "I didn't have a chance to tell you. Marcus said Wyndham knew this place when he

241

was young, but before it was a school – he knew the family that lived here. And as Marcus pointed out, it's been a school since the mid-nineteenth century."

Eloise was wide-eyed as she said, "And the family that lived here . . ."

"Was my family. I have to allow for the possibility that Wyndham's determination to destroy me is as much personal as a simple fight between good and evil."

"Oh, I'd say it's personal," said Marcus. "He told me that destroying you was his life's work." He turned to Eloise and said, "That's not normal, is it, talking like that?"

Eloise laughed and said, "No, I don't suppose it is." She looked at Will then, her expression full of meaning as she said, "Should we tell Marcus about our progress so far, what we've learned, or is it best he doesn't know?"

Will had no doubt that Marcus could be trusted – he was as sure of it as he was unsure of Chris and Rachel – and if anything, he suspected the more Marcus knew the more he would be wedded to their cause.

"Yes, tell him everything. I'm just going to look in the crypt."

"Do you want me to . . .?"

"No, I'm looking out of curiosity, nothing more. You tell Marcus our story."

Will started down the steps as Eloise began by saying,

"You know Will was born in 1240, right?"

The gentle murmur of her voice escorted him through the gate at the bottom of the steps, into the small crypt, more fitting than the chapel above for the family it was built to serve. Another room opened off it, housing slightly less ornate tombs, and beyond that, an ossuary, the door to which was locked.

He opened it and stepped inside. It was a small room, but the bones were piled high, skulls filling every wall from floor to ceiling, with other bones slotted in between as if to complete the decorative effect. Will couldn't understand where these bones had come from.

There was no churchyard nearby from which they would have needed to be removed. Nor had the land this house occupied been a burial ground. Will thought back to his youthful memories of Marland and was certain this area had been meadows back then.

He moved about the room, and saw now that many of the skulls were damaged, possibly broken as they were excavated, but equally possibly suggesting death in combat. He wondered if these bones had been found in the ground during the building work, the remains of some much more ancient burial site.

He stepped outside and locked the door again, then walked slowly around the two rooms of the crypt, feeling the walls, listening to the sounds of his own steps on the floor, trying to get a sense of whether some other chamber was hidden here, but finding nothing.

When he came back up into the chapel, Eloise stopped talking and looked at him, her expression asking if everything was OK. Will smiled and said, "There's a small room at the back of the crypt that's locked – it would be a convenient place for me to hide during daylight hours if I need to."

"So you won't go back to the new house?"

"Yes, but perhaps not today." He looked at Marcus and said, "How much of our story is left to tell?"

"Eloise just told me about Asmund – Wyndham never mentioned anything about that, not to me. I don't think he mentioned Lorcan . . .?"

"Labraid," said Eloise.

"Yeah, I don't think he's mentioned him."

Will said, "Unfortunately the trail has gone cold since I killed Asmund. We came here, and judging by Wyndham's efforts to thwart us, we've come to the right place, but in truth he would be as well served in leaving us alone because we have no idea where to turn next and no one to tell us."

"What do you mean, no one to tell you?"

Will looked at Eloise, but she said, "No, you tell him the last of it."

"Asmund has a master, and that master himself serves

Lorcan Labraid. Though I had never met another of my kind until I met Asmund, it seems others like me have gone to great lengths to protect me and ensure my comfort all these centuries. Yet now, when I need guidance most, none of them is to be seen."

Marcus laughed, loud enough that Eloise looked concerned, fearing the heavy chapel door might not contain that much noise. He jumped up from the pew then, unable to restrain himself, and stood on the altar step along from where Eloise sat.

"You know why they haven't shown themselves? Wyndham!"

"I don't understand. What has he done that would . . ."

"He's caught them – a few of them anyway."

"Caught?" Eloise said, standing up too.

"Caught! He's got them locked up in his cellars. I saw two of them, no three, and one of them talks all the time about you, telling him where you are, stuff like that."

Will and Eloise looked at each other. If she saw the implication of that last comment, she didn't let on. But Will realised he might have done Chris and Rachel a terrible injustice in not trusting them. If a captive vampire was giving Wyndham information, he hardly needed Chris to do the same.

"So Wyndham will know I'm here now."

"Not for sure – this vampire's half crazy because of

the stuff he does to them, because they don't get any blood. I guarantee right now it's shouting 'Marland' again and again. That's what it does."

"Then what hope have we if Asmund's master is half-crazed?"

Marcus shook his head. "I doubt that one's Asmund's master. There's another one, but he keeps it in a separate room and he wouldn't let me see it – said it was too dangerous."

Will said, "It?"

"Wyndham often calls them it, like they're animals, and some of them don't look human. Not you though; he always refers to you as he. So yeah, he wouldn't let me see it, said it was best I didn't." He looked from Will to Eloise and back again. "Well, what do you reckon? Maybe the one that's hidden away is the one you're looking for, and that's why no one's paid you a visit."

Will's thoughts were reeling. His destiny had not been hidden from him or made difficult on purpose. It was Wyndham at every turn, determined to stop him, to destroy him or keep him locked within this eternal torment.

It raised another question though. All along Wyndham had acted as if he feared an encounter with Will himself, always sending spirits and demons, turning nature against him, trying to kill Eloise, yet apparently he had no fear of vampires at all. If he had imprisoned Asmund's master, it seemed unlikely he would be fearful of Will.

"I don't understand," said Will. "If Wyndham has captured other vampires, why does he not engage me in direct combat? Why all these sorcerer's tricks, why attack Eloise, when he has it within his power to fight and triumph over my kind?"

"Because you're not just another vampire," said Eloise. "You're William of Mercia and Lorcan Labraid calls to you, not to anyone else, to you. Think about it. You shouldn't have been able to defeat Asmund – he was bigger than you and stronger – but you killed him. Wyndham isn't afraid of vampires, he's afraid of you."

"She's right," said Marcus.

Will wasn't convinced, but there was no question. If Wyndham had imprisoned vampires, they had to find where he lived, to take the battle to him at last, to give him something to fear.

"We have to find out where his house is."

"That's easy," said Marcus. "I know where it is."

"You said the windows of the car were blacked out."

"But I saw the house, and I know how far we drove, and I've lived around here my whole life. It's a mansion in the country on the other side of the city – I recognised it right away, saw it from the school bus once when we were on a trip."

Will nodded, imagining this house. His mind flew, away across the city with the cathedral spire standing proud, back out into the darkness with the snow falling in heavy flakes, seeing a house, perhaps as large as this, a house holding a secret. That secret, he thought, was not imprisoned vampires, but Wyndham's fear. He feared William of Mercia, and now Will was determined he would give him something to base that fear upon.

25

*T*o my great frustration, and though I encountered his victims often enough, I failed to find William of Mercia. I knew from my mother's description that he was a boy, and I had some idea of what he looked like, but he eluded me. I sought his lair too, but all of my powers, all of the dark arts at my disposal, failed to reveal its location to me.

When the victims stopped appearing, for a month, three months, six, I began to fear he'd gone into hibernation, denying me for decades more. And each time a new victim appeared, I rejoiced that he was active again, knowing also that I had gained so much new knowledge while he'd slept.

One thing I had realised early on was that it was not enough for me to kill vampires because there would always be more. To destroy the evil they represented I had to understand them, and to do that I had to capture and study them.

William of Mercia may have eluded me, but over

the course of the nineteenth and twentieth centuries I caught many of his kind. Some were from the wider area surrounding this city, for this seems a region particularly plagued by them, and others from across these islands.

I learned many hard lessons in those early days. I learned, for example, that the best way of transporting them was in a sealed box during the daytime – after all, why would they wish to escape into the agony of sunlight?

Equally, and almost to my great cost, I learned that as well as superhuman strength, they were possessed of the ability to open locks with the use of their minds alone. After much trial and error, I developed an ingenious system in which chains held their cages shut, but the chains fed through the floor and were locked in another room.

The bars and chains were made from a particularly strong alloy of my own design, but as knowledge of electricity developed in the early nineteenth century, I soon learned that I could run a current through the metal, strong enough to convince the captives that it was better not to touch the bars.

I won't dispute that some of the experiments I've carried out on these demons have not been pleasant. How else was I to learn how they lived and how they died? Fire and sunlight I soon discovered would make them plead for death, but would not kill them. Fire and light, I also learned, would make them talk.

Yet much of what I learned early on was gained without resorting to such methods. The second vampire I caught, in 1842, was unearthed in the south-west of England, a gentlemanly creature who insisted on being known only as Baal. A scholar in his first youth, he considered it amusing to be known now by the name of one of the Princes of Hell, for that is what he believed he'd become.

He still had the look of a young student with dreams of following in the footsteps of the late Lord Byron, yet Baal had actually been alive since the time of Chaucer. Born in 1360, he'd been lucky enough to be taken under the tutelage of the vampire who'd infected him. It speaks of both Baal's sense of honour and his ruthlessness that he'd killed his master as soon as he'd learned everything the latter could impart.

It was Baal who told me that they only fed on those who did not carry the vampire bloodline, and even then only on those who were fit and healthy. It was the life force they were taking from their victims, spiritual nourishment rather than food, and the life remaining within a body determined how long it would be before they needed blood again.

Garlic, he told me, was not repugnant to them, but confused their otherwise extraordinary senses, making it impossible to judge the blood of potential victims. The crucifix meant nothing to them, and Baal, a committed and penitent believer himself, reasoned this was because his condition predated the arrival of Christianity.

Daylight and fire were like the agonies of Hell, and a stake through the heart would weaken them to the extent of helplessness, but Baal also confirmed that I had quite accidentally chanced upon the only certain way of killing a vampire – the removal of its head.

Of course, I did not entirely take Baal's word for all these things and carried out experiments over the following decades to test the truth of them. He was never the subject of these himself, and I must admit that for all the evil he carried within him, I respected him, even liked him.

In 1861, desperate for blood, he begged me to end his life. He had been reading almost continuously for months before this, the Bible most often of all, even though I tried to discourage him from a book which I've never found of worth.

I agreed, albeit with a sad heart, and before the end I asked if he would at last tell me his real name.

"I cannot use it," he said. "It would bring shame on the good people who gave it to me." I nodded and

he said, "I'm ready," and closed his eyes.

Another demon in an adjoining cage had never seen his own kind's death, and the sight of Baal disappearing so completely filled him with such horror that he began to babble. How ironic that it was an act of mercy on my part that should lead to the greatest leap in my knowledge.

It still took the application of bright lights to get the facts reasonably straight, but it was this creature that told me of Lorcan Labraid, a demon it laughably described as the overlord of all vampires, a vampire king. Even under extreme torture, it claimed not to know the whereabouts of this greater demon, but it did admit to knowing where I could find Labraid's servant, the demon that did his bidding. Was this William of Mercia, I asked, because I had heard the name by now and reasoned it was the one I sought.

"William of Mercia?" The creature laughed through its pain. "It's not for the likes of me to know about William of Mercia. But the vampire I speak of is more powerful than anything you'll have yet encountered."

This was intriguing, but once again I couldn't persuade it to talk further on the subject, even when I threatened to remove its head, a threat I eventually carried out. In the face of such obstinacy or ignorance, the only inference I could take was that even the vampire king, Lorcan Labraid, waited on William of Mercia.

I had neither of them, but I had precise information on the whereabouts of Labraid's loyal lieutenant. The location was close by, deep beneath a mausoleum in one of the city's oldest cemeteries. If it had not been for the information I'd received, I would not have believed the mausoleum to contain any hidden passages and I certainly could not find the entrance.

But in much the same way as we'd captured that first vampire many years before, I surrounded the mausoleum at dusk with a handful of servants, their lanterns covered so as not to give away our position.

The small stone building had a circular window high up facing the door and this window had broken at some point in the past. The plan was that, when I gave the word, one of the servants would lift the kitchen boy up to that broken window and he would drop a burning torch inside with the aim of flushing the demon out – I knew it would be able to sense us outside and did not want it to retreat deep underground.

A little after nightfall I heard stone slabs moving within the mausoleum. A stillness followed, and this I knew from experience was the demon testing the air. I signalled and the boy was lifted up to the window. He looked briefly horrified, and for a moment, I feared he would lose his nerve, but with admirable precision, he threw the burning torch into the building.

The scream which resulted was so alarming that I saw my servants becoming agitated, but they had no time to think on what was coming. An instant later, the demon emerged, wild and vicious and terrifying. Even in the painful glare of our lamps, it lashed out and I think if we'd been relying on light alone, we wouldn't have succeeded.

But the demon had failed to notice that it had emerged on to a small wooden platform and now, at my command, four sides of a cage sprang up round the creature, a fifth falling into place on the roof. The process was so fast that there was no longer any question that the demon would end up in my cellars.

Little did I know that this was the point at which my progress with this particular fiend was to end. Usually when caught, the creatures spend the first days testing the bars and exploring their surroundings like a spider trying to escape an upturned glass.

As if sensing immediately that there was no escape, this demon sat and fell deep into some sort of trance from which it could not be shaken. It was as if it was deep in communication with itself, or with another far away.

I burned its flesh and it did not flinch, I even used mirrors to expose it to sunlight, and though its flesh combusted, still the demon did not respond. The flesh healed and I tried again, but always without response. Nor over the many decades that followed did it ever give any indication of a spiritual hunger from the lack of blood.

I knew full well that this was a demon of a different order, and even though it failed to yield any further information, I became convinced that if this strikingly strong and powerful demon answered to Lorcan Labraid, then maybe he was indeed a vampire king.

For nearly one hundred and fifty years I have held this demon captive, longer than any of the others, and in all that I time I had never heard it speak, nor seen any other signs to suggest it was even fully conscious. Then last November, as I worked nearby, it suddenly uttered five words, quite clearly.

So surprised was I that I couldn't be certain I had heard correctly. But I noticed the demon's eyes were open, and it seemed to smile as it repeated the words, "William of Mercia rises again."

I walked over and asked it what it meant by those words, but nothing more was forthcoming, the trance was re-established, and I knew better than to waste time on more torture.

This creature was evil, and it waited upon evil in the form of Lorcan Labraid, and Lorcan Labraid waited *upon evil in the form of William of Mercia. I knew this was not just the end of another hibernation for my mother's tormentor, but that something momentous was afoot and that if good was to triumph, I would need to prepare for battle. This, I realised, was the point to which I'd been heading, and for which I hoped my long education had prepared me.*

26

E loise walked a couple of paces ahead of him, then stopped and turned, smiling. The sun was behind her, catching her hair, outlining the curves of her body through the material of her summer blouse.

"I could tell you things about this place that you don't know."

"Then tell me," Will said.

She reached out and took his hands, her warmth radiating through him, and lowered herself to sit on the grass, pulling him to the ground too. A memory flashed into Will's mind, of lowering Alex Shawcross to the floor in the same way, but he fought to stop it from taking over.

"Take the grass we're sitting on." He looked down at it, a vibrant sunlit green that filled him with heartache. "There are thousands of bodies buried under it, all over here."

"How so?"

She said, "They found hundreds when they built

the old house, more when they built the new one, but they're everywhere. They think a huge battle took place here in ancient times, but it was a burial site too, for pagan warriors and kings."

"I should've known that," he said, but he was distracted now by her lips, soft, slightly parted, inviting. He leaned forward and kissed her and reached out to hold her, but his hand failed to find the warmth of her body and the dream melted away.

Will opened his eyes, disappointed, and stared at the wall of skulls which stared blankly back at him. He was sitting cross-legged, his back against the ossuary door. He wondered if his location had inspired the dream or if the dream had answered for all these remains.

Marland had been a place of significance long before the abbey had been built there, that much was obvious to him. It had been common too for churches to be built on sites that had been of significance to their pagan predecessors.

So a sacred place for the burial of warriors and kings seemed likely. But the site of a large battle too? There had been no talk of this being a battlefield during Will's childhood, or at least nothing that had been spoken of in front of him. If there had been a battle here, it could only have been in ancient times.

He stood and looked at one of the skulls, running his

hand across the time-darkened facial bones, up towards the jagged fracture on one side of the forehead. And he wondered what this warrior would have been able to tell him of this place and what had happened here.

Will was distracted for a moment, sensing that the sun had set in the world above, but he turned back to the skull and stared a few moments longer, trying to imagine the man this had been, saying finally, "Little do you know how much I envy you."

He turned and left the ossuary, though he delayed for another hour or so in the crypt. He listened to the school choir as it practised above, and at the end, he heard the supervising teacher mention something about the appointment of a new chaplain. They filed out afterwards, chattering, happy, and the lights were turned out and the heavy door closed.

A little while later, Will climbed the steps. The combination of the moon behind snow clouds and the snow itself on the ground outside produced an ethereal light that made him feel homesick for his own church again, a homesickness that represented everything he had lost and longed to get back, even as he knew it would never be in his power again.

He sat in one of the pews, losing track of time. When he heard someone approaching, he moved quickly and descended halfway down the steps into the crypt. The door opened and closed, but rather than the lights coming on, a torch beam bounced across the dark interior of the chapel.

A moment later, he heard Eloise say, "Will?"

He put on his dark glasses, not confident of them managing to keep the torch beams under control, and climbed the steps again.

"I'm here."

They both had torches and walked towards him now, going to great lengths to keep the beams on the floor in front of them. Marcus was carrying a rucksack and Eloise held some rolled-up papers under her arm.

She said, "We've brought candles – there are still a lot of people about so we thought it might make more sense to go to the crypt."

"Good thinking," said Will and walked back down the steps ahead of them.

He waited then while Eloise and Marcus lit some candles on one of the flat-topped tombs in the second chamber. Once there was enough light for them to see, they turned off the torches and Will removed his glasses.

Marcus looked around the room and said, "You spent the whole day down here? You don't sleep?"

"I don't sleep at all. And I spent most of the day in there." He pointed at the old wooden door to the ossuary. "It's the nature of my condition – one gets used to being alone."

Marcus nodded, accepting the comment at face value. "I suppose we're all alone one way or another."

"Cheery," said Eloise, then pointed and said, "What's in there anyway?"

"It's full of human bones. There was a battle here long ago, the ground all around is full of human remains."

Eloise looked surprised and said, "How amazing. I've never heard anything about that."

Will wasn't sure why he took such perverse satisfaction from proving his dream wrong and said only, "It's not a widely known fact."

"Well, maybe it should be." She smiled. "Anyway, we've had a productive day. The place we're looking for is called Southerton House, a couple of miles outside the city, but on the other side from us. Marcus recognised the picture straight away. And it's owned by a company based in the Cayman Islands, which is obviously one of Wyndham's fronts."

She spread out a map of the area on the top of the tomb and pointed to where the house was, then placed a photograph next to it, printed off the internet. Will looked at them, but didn't think he'd ever seen the house, even on his longer nocturnal walks. Seeing the map and how little of it he'd covered made him realise how confined his world was. For the most part, since the time of his sickness, he had stirred little beyond the city itself, particularly as the edges of the city had crept out into the countryside.

He turned to Marcus and said, "What sort of defences does he have?"

"You mean security?" He got a nod from Eloise and said, "Probably cameras on the gates and walls, but I didn't see them. He told me there were attack dogs in the grounds and I bet the house is alarmed."

"Not very much to contend with," said Will, and wondered if Wyndham was a little too confident that his house would not be found, and that his sorcery would be enough to protect it if it were. Not that Will underestimated Wyndham's magical powers. He turned to Marcus. "I know I need not ask Eloise, but I ask you, do you want to be part of this? There will be unknown dangers and it will place your break with Wyndham beyond repair."

"Oh, I'm coming. I'm done with Wyndham, I told you that, and besides, you need me there."

"So be it," said Will. "You have torches which, as Eloise knows well, are as useful a weapon as any. We have the sabres." He looked at Marcus and said, "He will have told you, but I tell you again, avoid eye contact with them. If you stab them through the heart, they are weakened but not killed. The only way of killing them is to sever the head."

Even as he spoke, he realised he was talking about "them" instead of "us" and Marcus appeared to pick up on that and said, "Hold on, I thought the vampires were on your side. I thought that's why we're going there, so that they can tell you stuff."

"That is my hope, but you say these poor creatures have been locked up, possibly for decades or more, starved of blood, driven half-mad. I sincerely hope Asmund's master is more helpful than he was himself, but the others could be very dangerous indeed."

"Yeah, they're in some pretty serious cages, but I get what you're saying."

Will looked at Eloise and said, "I'll try to obtain a weapon for you, or you . . ."

Before he finished she said, "I'll take a torch, but I'm not chopping anyone's head off, so it's better that I don't – I'll end up dropping it or something, or stabbing myself with it."

"Fine. All that remains then is to plan a time. Is tomorrow night convenient?"

They looked at each other and Eloise said, "As good as any. About eleven o'clock? How are we getting there? Do you want me to call Rachel and Chris?"

"No, we'll take a taxi. I see no way of them helping

in this, so I see no point in endangering them." She appeared satisfied with that, and certainly didn't seem to think it was a matter of trust. And for once, it wasn't, but rather a practical decision. "Good. We'll meet here tomorrow."

Marcus looked enthusiastic, but said, "Great, but I've got to go. I've got a chess match waiting for me."

"I'll catch you up," said Eloise.

Marcus flashed her a cheeky, knowing grin, gave his now familiar wave to Will, even though he was standing within reach of him, and left, skipping up the steps of the crypt.

Eloise waited until she heard the door to the chapel open and close and looked at Will questioningly. Will nodded, assuring her that Marcus had left, and she said, "You do trust him?"

"Do you?"

It looked as if it pained her to admit it, but she said, "Yes, I do actually. I mean, I've only really got to know him today and even then I've only spent a couple of hours with him, but I really like him. He's smart and he's funny." The doubts crept back into her face though. "It's just, he was working for Wyndham as recently as yesterday and this is all just a bit too convenient, him knowing where the house is, telling us about the prisoners, and we're about to follow him in there – it could be a trap."

Will thought about it before saying, "It could be that Wyndham is setting a trap right now, that he's been planning one all along in the certainty that I would eventually find him. But I have absolutely no doubt that Marcus Jenkins is trustworthy. I knew it, somehow, even when he was working for Wyndham, and I don't know why that is."

"I hope you're right. Because I do like him, Will." Eloise looked at her watch and said, "I'll have to go soon as well." But she didn't move and a moment later, she said, "The way we were last night, before the . . . whatever it was that happened in the new house. I don't ever want us to be like that again. And I know you have to feed, but you have to understand that it's difficult for me, that it'll take me a while to accept it for what it is."

"I do."

"Good." She thought about it a little more and said, "I think Wyndham got under my skin more than I realised, not so much with the attacks, more with what he made me see in the tunnels."

"I know, and I wish you didn't have to contend with such things. I wish for your sake above all that I could be like any other boy, I really do." She shook her head, but he said, "I dreamt about you today."

"What did you dream?"

"I dreamt we were sitting in a meadow here, in the sun, and you told me about the battle fought here long ago and the bones that lay under the grass." She smiled, understanding his comment about the ossuary earlier. "And we kissed, just a normal kiss, the likes of which I can remember now only in my dreams. We were young and in love and the sun was shining – is that too much to ask or hope for?"

Eloise shook her head, but didn't speak, only moved closer and held on to him, burying her head into his shoulder. He held her back, stroking her hair, releasing the blossom smell of it that was itself a reminder of another summer.

"Do you dream of me?"

She held him tighter, a reflex response, and her voice was muffled as she said, "All the time." He could feel the heat of her mouth through his shirt, her heart beating against his chest.

"Good dreams or bad dreams?"

She laughed this time as she said, "Good dreams."

She pulled away then, but reached up, holding his face in her hands as she said, "Maybe you have those dreams for a reason. You know, maybe your destiny is that you'll be cured of this, that you'll . . ." She stopped, perhaps struggling to believe it herself.

And he smiled. She had to go now, he knew that,

but she dreamt of him, and he had learned a long time ago to take comfort where he might, so he would take comfort in that.

27

As the taxi driver pulled to the side of the road, he said, "You don't need to get back tonight I hope? The way this snow's coming down I don't see any cars getting along this road later."

"We'll be fine, thank you."

The driver looked beyond the metal gates, the house just visible in the darkness, and only then because it was framed in snow.

"You sure you don't want to check they're in first? I can't see any lights on."

Will was in the passenger seat and as the other two got out, he smiled at the driver and said, "How much do we owe you?"

By the time he joined them, Marcus had unwrapped the sabres from the black shawl they were in. Eloise took the shawl from him and tied it round her neck.

They stood there for a moment, gathering snow, as the taxi lumbered around in a big circle and started back towards the city, the car itself hinting at its driver's confusion. As the tail lights disappeared, the three of them approached the gates which were locked by way of a heavy chain.

Eloise pointed and said, "That's what you'd do if you were going away for a while, don't you think? You wouldn't lock it like that if you were inside."

"Perhaps not," said Will. "But if Wyndham isn't at home, it will make our main business here all the easier."

Will took hold of the chain and snapped it apart, the two broken halves of the link flying away into the snow. He took a sabre from Marcus and said, "Stay close to me whenever possible." He looked at Eloise as he added, "I don't want to make the same mistake I made last time."

She nodded and he pushed open the gate, closing it again once all three of them were inside. As Marcus had suggested, there were cameras on the top of the gateposts, and though they looked inactive, it hardly mattered to Will if Wyndham knew they were here. Even if he didn't, he would know soon enough.

The drive was lost in the single smooth expanse of snow that covered the parkland, suggesting no car had driven here in at least two days. They took the most direct route to the house and were halfway there when Will stopped and listened. The other two stopped with him and then he moved around them, gesturing for them to stand back.

They were not visible yet, but he could hear two dogs, then a third, running towards them. They didn't bark, but when they became visible, three black, muscular shapes pounding through the snow towards them, their intent was clear enough.

Marcus said, "I'll take the one on the left if you can do the other two."

Will smiled, certain they'd found a fine ally in Marcus Jenkins, but he said, "There will be no need for that, trust me."

The dogs were bearing down on them now, teeth bared, eyes focused. All at once, the three of them appeared to pick Will out as their target and, all at once, they became aware of his stare. They stopped quite suddenly, one of them stumbling in the snow, righting itself in a panic.

They stared in confusion and the first hint of fear. One tested a growl, but immediately followed it by slinking down to the ground and shuffling backwards. Will continued to stare out at them, and all three were backing away now, before finally they turned, and ran back to the side of the house, not in fear, but as if they could no longer remember why they had run out there.

"They won't trouble us again," said Will and carried on towards the house.

Marcus laughed. "Where I come from, you could make a lot of money with a trick like that."

Eloise laughed too, but then said, "We didn't ask you how you got to the cellars – is there a side door or something?"

"No, I went from the main hall inside the house. We went through the front door."

Will said, "Then that's what we'll do tonight."

They reached the imposing Georgian façade and climbed the steps between stone columns. They stood there, under the portico, as they brushed the snow from their coats and hair.

Will had his back to the door as he did this, looking out at the fresh snow adding to the soft, white mantle that already covered the world, the new flakes erasing their footsteps as he watched. For a fleeting moment, he allowed himself the same little fantasy, that the thaw would come and reveal the world as he had known it long ago.

"Will, are you ready?" He turned, and smiled to see Eloise's face, her beautiful eyes, her pale cheeks with a slight bloom of red on them from the cold. He wouldn't want a thaw that revealed a world without her.

"I'm ready."

He approached the two wooden doors, a large metal doorknob on each. He was about to put his hands on to get a sense of the mechanism, but he hesitated, his hearing picking up something indistinct, coming from the doors themselves. He stepped closer, listening without making contact.

"He knows the power I have over locks. There is a current running through these doors – if I touch the handles, I'll be electrocuted."

Marcus said, "He uses electricity to keep the vampires under control."

Will nodded and said, "That answers that question. Electricity must hurt us the same way light does."

Eloise said, "You didn't know that already?"

"I'm lucky enough never to have been struck by lightning or electrocuted by accident – it never occurred to me to try it on purpose."

Marcus said, "But if you can't do your stuff on the locks, how do we get in?"

Will took a step back and planted the sole of his foot between the two handles with a fierce kick. The doors cracked apart and burst open, one of them looking as if it might come off its hinges, then rebounded before opening a second time and staying open.

Will stepped forward into the marble expanse of the hall, and Eloise and Marcus followed in after him. They turned on their torches, but aimed them to the sides of the room, subduing the beams enough for Will not to be troubled by them.

Marcus pointed at the large staircase rising up directly ahead and said, "The door to the cellars is round the back of the main staircase, to the right."

They walked in that direction and Eloise said, "Marcus, there's something I've been meaning to say to you. Whatever happens tonight, as soon as we get back to school . . ." She paused for effect. "We're going to stretch your jumper – doesn't it bother you that it fits so well?"

Marcus laughed a little, but said, "After tonight, I don't think my scholarship's likely to be good for much longer."

"Then we'll find another way, won't we, Will? You have to stay at Marland now."

Will turned and offered a smile of encouragement, which appeared to cheer Marcus, though Will couldn't quite imagine how he could secure Marcus's education. Will stared for a moment longer at the two of them then, impressed by the thought that this union had always been meant to take place, as if Marcus too was part of his destiny.

Eloise said, "What's up?"

"Nothing," said Will. "Only it feels right that the three of us are here together."

"I agree," said Marcus. "You might laugh at me, but that night by the river, I felt like I'd been waiting for that moment my whole life."

Eloise smiled at him, touched, as she said, "Other people might laugh at that, but they don't know the things we know."

"Indeed," said Will, and pushed open the door that led to the cellar steps.

His mood became instantly more serious. He could hear someone shouting, beyond the reach of Eloise and Marcus's hearing, but he could hear it quite clearly, a frightened, almost hysterical cry.

"He's here! He's here! He's here," repeated again and again.

28

They moved quickly down the steps, then along the short corridor at the bottom, which ended at a heavy metal door. There was no current running through this one, nor was there a normal lock, only three large bolts.

Even Marcus and Eloise could hear the cry from inside now, and Marcus whispered, "That's the one that talks – he's like that all the time."

"He's here! He's here!"

To Will's ears the cries had become deafening.

They pulled the bolts open and stepped into the room. Marcus closed the door behind them as Will stood, getting used to the subdued light in there, taking in everything he could see.

Other rooms led off it, but this was a cavernous cellar, with all manner of instruments, electrical devices, chemistry apparatus, specimens in jars along one wall. It was like the mad scientist's laboratory of storybooks. The far side of the room was filled with a cage structure, split into four, though with solid metal walls separating them from each other.

One cage, on the far right, was empty. The one on the far left housed the vampire who shouted. He was sitting in the middle of the enclosure, his mind apparently quite unhinged, but looking remarkably healthy. His clothes looked of the nineteenth century and were shabby, but his hair was fair and appeared to have been cut, and his face was that of a man in his twenties, no more. Only the madness in his eyes spoke of the blood-hunger.

The creatures in the other two cages were very different, and creatures was the only word Will could find appropriate. They pounced towards the bars at the sight of Marcus and Eloise, immediately being thrown back by an electric shock, and then punished further by spotlights that came on and beamed at them for a few seconds, both vampires screaming and trying to shield their eyes.

Their clothes were torn and burned so badly that it was impossible to say in which era they'd originated. Their hair had grown wild and matted. Worst of all, their faces and hands bore terrible burns. It was clear that Wyndham had experimented on them, tortured them, learning what it was that could damage them. The end result was that these creatures now looked as if they had never been human.

As soon as the spotlights turned off, and despite the recent pain, they immediately started pacing back and forth in the cages, as if building up to another attempt on the bars.

"He's here! He's here! He's here!"

All three had long fangs, the ferocious appearance of which only served to make the vampires look all the more pathetic in their cages. They were like exotic wild animals being paraded for public amusement in a forgotten zoo.

Eloise looked sickened and disturbed by the sight. Marcus, who'd seen it before, pointed at a door to the left of the cages and said, "The other one is through there, but Wyndham didn't let me go in there."

Will nodded and looked at the empty cage. A creature had been kept in there too, he imagined. He felt no particular empathy for these creatures, and had been so alone for so long that he struggled even to think of them as fellow sufferers of the same sickness, but he was saddened to think of how many creatures might have been tortured to death in Wyndham's search for knowledge.

Will waved the sabre towards the cages and said, "I suspect we'll learn little from these. If Asmund's master is beyond that door, that's where we should begin."

They started to move across the room, but were

brought to a halt within a step or two as a loud buzzing noise sounded, almost but not quite drowned out by the repeated shouts of the vampire on the left.

The noise stopped again, and then, surprisingly, so did the vampire. He looked about himself, puzzled by some development. The other two continued to pace back and forth, sniffing at the air, edging towards the bars at the front and then back again.

Will, Eloise and Marcus stared at the cages, listened – silence – and then finally Eloise said, "Marcus, do you know what that noise was?"

He shook his head, mystified, but started cautiously towards the cages as he said, "I think he turned the current off."

Sure enough, the two creatures grabbed hold of the bars and started, with some effort, to bend them. They jumped back from them again as another brief buzzing sounded, but then, with no further warning, the doors of all four cages slid open.

The vampire on the left remained seated as before, staring in silent confusion. The other two needed no further encouragement. They leapt from the cages. One made for Marcus, fangs already bared, a violent need for life, and now out of the cage they could see he was tall, and Marcus insignificant in front of him.

It was over with astonishing speed. Suddenly a light

shone from Marcus's hand into the eyes of the creature. Its pace faltered and in that moment, Marcus's other hand swung round in a graceful arc, slicing through the creature's neck.

A blue light burst from the wound, as if that in itself had removed the head from its body, the entire form of the creature disappearing then in a brief dazzling pulse of energy. Marcus stumbled in surprise.

The other vampire had been rushing blindly towards Eloise, but it stopped, squinting in pain, then saw a tray of surgical instruments on a workbench in front of it. The memory of those implements appeared to fill it with hatred and it swiped them off the bench, sending them flying across the room towards Marcus.

Marcus fell backwards, dropping his sword, and tried to cover his face as the scalpels and drills crashed into him. He scrambled to get the weapon back, but the vampire was too fast. It jumped down to get the sabre, then swiped it through the air at all of them as it steadied itself. Marcus retreated cautiously around the edge of the room back towards Will and Eloise.

Will moved a little to the side so that Eloise was behind him, but then said, "Enough! There is no need for this, and no need for you to be afraid. I am William of Mercia and I give you my word that we mean you no harm."

"He's here," said a quiet voice from the cages, but only once.

"Ha!" The creature kicked a nearby table, sending it flying to the far wall where it smashed into the shelves of specimen jars. His fury was all the greater now. "If I'd known that, maybe I would have been spared this!" He gestured at the wounds on his face.

"He tortured you for information about me?"

"Tortured? You don't know how he tortured, thinking I lied to protect you." He laughed, a pained, bitter laugh. "I don't know who you are, I don't care, and I would've taken you to him on a stake myself if he'd let me go."

"He is the one," said the quiet voice behind. "From four will come one. He's here."

The creature didn't risk turning, but shouted, "Shut! Up!"

Marcus had completed his cautious retreat and was alongside Eloise now.

"Sorry I lost the sword."

Will heard Eloise say, "You were amazing, quite simply amazing."

"I agree," said Will.

The creature looked at him and said, "I agree too, with whatever nonsense it is you discuss. Now, William of Mercia, as you're here . . . why don't you get out of my way."

His meaning was clear.

Eloise's voice sounded close, her breath falling hot on Will's neck as she said, "We'll both shine our torches at him at once."

"Not this time," said Will. "When this starts, move over to the door. Should I lose, get out of that door and bolt it – it will give you a little time. Now stand back."

The creature stared at him, trying to decipher what was going on, showing enough intelligence to keep his craving under control, though Will could easily imagine the agonies he had to be in.

Will said, "Do you have a name?"

"I am not an animal, as you well know. Why does it concern you?"

"It's a common courtesy, in such circumstances, to know the names of those you kill."

"A valid point. But then I already know yours."

He lunged forward, holding his sword out wide, ready to swing it round towards Will's head. And in the depth of the creature's blood-famine, he had failed to notice that his opponent was left-handed. Will stepped nimbly to the right and struck the creature's neck with such force that the blue light itself exploded across the room, licking round the broken specimen jars before disappearing.

"He's here," said a quiet voice.

Will crouched down and picked up the sword, still touched with flashes of blue light, and held it out for Marcus to take. Marcus and Eloise hadn't even moved towards the door, but then Will was surprised himself at the speed with which he'd dispatched the creature.

He smiled and said, "That was easier than I thought." He looked at Marcus. "And I agree with Eloise – your skill with a sword is remarkable. You have never been trained?"

Marcus shrugged. "I didn't think about what I was doing really. Just instinct, I suppose."

"He's here."

They turned back to the third vampire who remained sitting on the floor, ignoring the open door of his cage.

Will was about to speak when a strange noise tore through the cellar, coming from the room beyond, a sound like metal being wrenched apart. There was a shuddering smash and the ground beneath their feet seemed to shake with the impact. The last of the bottles and jars fell to the floor and shattered. A second crash followed, and dust fell from the ceiling above them.

They all looked at the door to the neighbouring room, where Marcus had said Asmund's master might be. Only the vampire in the cage seemed oblivious. A moment later, the door was torn away from its hinges and thrown across the room as if a bomb had been planted behind it.

As the noise faded, a rustling could be heard in the corridor beyond, and Will could hear the soft fall of footsteps. They stared, all three of them, waiting, knowing that this creature had not been released, but had apparently chosen its moment to break free.

None of them expected what followed. Asmund's master, or so it seemed, emerged slowly and with care, as if still getting used to walking after a long confinement. But Asmund's master was a woman. Will could only assume Asmund had spoken of a master because he hadn't wanted to admit that he'd served and had been bitten by a woman.

She was tall, wearing a long, black dress which had gathered dust. Her hair was red and fell in waves down her back. She was ghostly and slender and sternly beautiful. As she emerged, she looked down at the vampire in the cage.

"He's here," he said.

Her voice when she spoke had the kindly but superior tone of a lady speaking to a loyal servant, "I hear you – hush now."

She turned slowly to look across the room and the moment she saw Will she let out a single laugh, exposing gleaming white fangs. She appeared overjoyed and speechless at the sight of him.

Almost instantly though, she grew concerned and said, "My Lord, you should not have come here. This is the sorcerer's lair."

"The sorcerer is not here, and besides, I do not fear him."

She laughed again, beaming with what appeared to be pride.

"But My Lord, I would have come to you when the time was right." She closed her eyes for a moment, before saying, "There is much to tell, and much to be done, but first, as is custom, I will accept your offerings with gratitude."

Will stared at her in surprise, and only realised too late what it was she thought had been brought as offerings. She reached out a hand and Eloise screamed and flew across the room towards her, falling stunned into her grasp.

Marcus let out a cry and stepped forward immediately. Will didn't move, but shouted, "Stop!"

He had sensed rightly that this woman looked upon him with some degree of awe. She still held Eloise close to her, but she looked at Will as if trying to understand his anger.

"These people have not been brought as offerings,

and I forbid you to treat them as such."

The lady smiled sweetly and spoke with a pleasant voice that Will mistrusted.

"My Lord, I am Elfleda. Was I not his queen? Indeed, I am still his queen, as I will be until your time is come. Do you not think then, My Lord, that it is appropriate to bring me offerings?"

He recalled the torment this queen – Elfleda, whose name he had not known until now – had inflicted upon Asmund from a distance. He reasoned that it was better to pacify her than to argue with her.

"That is so, and forgive me Elfleda, but this is Eloise, the girl of whom it is spoken in the prophecies."

She smiled again, as if there had been a misunder-standing, and then spoke as sweetly as she said, "Don't you think I know that?" There was only a fraction of a second in which to act, as she pulled Eloise towards her and opened her mouth to expose her fangs.

Will leapt forward, but Marcus was already closer and struck with lightning speed towards Elfleda's neck. Her reaction was even quicker, hurling Eloise aside, her body flying through the air and crashing into the broken shelves. At the same time, Elfleda raised her other arm and Marcus spun and flew into it just as Eloise had.

It didn't deter him and still he tried to raise his sword, but she responded with a vicious animal snap, like a dog lashing out, biting his hand and forcing him to drop the sabre. She held him in front of her body like a shield, forcing Will to hold his ground.

"What misunderstandings," said Elfleda sweetly, as if truly baffled by the turn of events.

She was quite calm, but appeared to be trying to think what she should do next. Marcus was in no doubt. Even held immobile, suspended in mid-air, his eyes caught Will's and looked down towards his other hand where he still held his torch. Will understood his meaning and nodded, preparing himself.

Marcus turned on the torch and raised it up, shining it back over his shoulder and into Elfleda's face. The beam hit her eyes and she grimaced as if irritated, but no more than that – she didn't so much as flinch from the pain. And then she braced her arms where they held Marcus and he screamed for a moment until a terrible cracking noise silenced him.

It all happened so quickly, Will hardly knew what had happened, but it was soon clear enough. Elfleda threw Marcus's body at Will's feet where it lay broken and crumpled. Will needed no superior senses to know that Marcus was dead.

The queen was furious now as she said, "You have been alone too long, it seems! Your destiny is great, My Lord, but not so great that you may disregard the weight of the history upon your shoulders." She looked across the room to where Eloise lay, and said, "Now, where were we – offerings, I think." She raised her hand slowly, ready to repeat the same act of magnetism she'd already performed.

Will didn't need to look at Eloise to know she was still alive, albeit unconscious. Nor did he need to look at Marcus, but he glanced down and saw his loyal eyes staring blankly, that ghost of a scar, and he felt hatred welling up inside him. This should not have ended like this. Marcus had been meant for greater things, had seemed part of this just as Eloise had, and yet now he was dead.

"Elfleda! You will hear me first!"

He stepped over Marcus's body and walked slowly towards the queen. She lowered her hand again, leaving Eloise where she was, and looked at Will. For a moment, for all her powers, it seemed as if she was mesmerised by him, puzzled, hurt and confused.

"My Queen, *here* is my offering."

She smiled, the same sweetly sinister smile, and it stayed on her lips as he drove his sabre with such force into her heart that only the hilt stopped his fist passing into her chest. She looked down then, not so much with surprise, but with the appearance of someone finally understanding a mystery that had long troubled her. She crumpled slowly to her knees, then fell back on to her haunches.

"My Lord," she said, but the words fell away in her mouth, as if the strength to speak had vanished too.

Will looked into her eyes and said quietly, "Why can you people not just help me? Why do you keep forcing me to do this by trying to take from me the one thing I will not relinquish?"

She stared back, silent.

"He's here," said a voice behind her.

Will crossed the room to Eloise and held her, helped her to sit up. She had been knocked unconscious, but was coming around now and she mumbled groggily and held the side of her chest.

"Eloise."

"I'm OK," she said hazily. "I hurt my head, and my ribs, I think. What about . . ."

"Marcus is dead."

Her eyes focused and she saw the body crumpled on the floor and tried involuntarily to push herself away from it, her legs pushing her back against the broken shelves, horrified that this could have happened in so short a space of time.

"No, he . . . but he . . ."

Will put his fingers on her lips, calming her, then said, "Stay here for now. There's something I must do."

He walked back and picked up the sabre that Marcus had briefly handled with such promise. Elfleda's eyes followed him and she looked up weakly as he stood in front of her. She could see the sword in his hand and nodded a little, understanding.

She spoke, her words barely more than a whisper, "How will you complete your journey if you continue to kill your guides?"

Will ignored her, positioning himself, focusing his hatred into the sabre in front of him. He looked at her and smiled, and for the last time she smiled back and said, "See, My Lord, this is how you become a king."

He swung and the vampire in the cage screamed. The blue light exploded around the room and the sabre that had been in Elfleda's chest fell to the floor. When Will was able to open his eyes, there was nothing left of her. A woman who had wielded such powers, and yet nothing whatsoever remained.

He looked across the room where Eloise had managed to get to her feet. She walked forward, carefully, testing herself out. Will went to meet her and held her, needing comfort as much as giving it because he had failed this time, he was certain of it, and Marcus had lost his life needlessly in the process.

When Eloise finally pulled away from him, tears streamed down her cheeks. He wiped them away and they both turned to look at Marcus's body. One leg was bent awkwardly underneath him, and though it meant little, Will couldn't help but go over and straighten it, giving him at least the appearance of someone at peace.

Will looked at his face again and said, "I meant to ask him and never did, how he got that scar."

"He . . ." Eloise started, but choked on the words and took a deep breath before saying, "He was born with it. He told me the other day. I mean yesterday. He told me yesterday. He was born with it."

Will nodded and knelt down and closed Marcus's eyes.

Eloise came up behind him. "What do we now, Will?"

Will stood and gestured at the vampire who was sitting meekly in his cage, rocking back and forth. "We talk to him."

A voice came suddenly from the fourth cage, saying, "Oh, he won't be able to tell you anything."

They turned, Will's grip tightening on the sabre, as a well-dressed, grey-haired man stepped from the previously empty enclosure and into the room.

29

The man was unarmed, but looked quite unconcerned as he said, "You know who I am, but for the sake of form, do allow me to introduce myself. My name is Phillip Wyndham." Will tensed, but Wyndham smiled. "Save your energy, William of Mercia. I'm not so foolish as to be here in person. This is merely an image and I am safely far away."

"Why do you wish to destroy me?"

"Because you're evil, because everything that will come from you is evil."

"That's a lie," shouted Eloise.

"And what would you know? What have you learned in your sixteen years that I have not in several centuries? I showed you the truth and you refused to believe it." His image looked real, but it appeared to face the wrong way now as it said, "As did poor Marcus. See what you did by bringing him here."

Will ignored his comment and walked to the door

of the cage in which the vampire sat and said, "Where is Lorcan Labraid?"

"He won't answer you," said Wyndham. "He has been conditioned to tell me where *you* are."

"Then why is he silent now?" It was true – the vampire had not uttered a single word since the death of the queen, and had failed to respond at all to Wyndham's apparition. Will saw what Wyndham clearly did not. "You are a fool, Wyndham. He was not informing you of anything, he was informing his queen, Elfleda. What vanity of yours to assume that your powers are greater than ours."

Wyndham laughed and called out, "Edgar, where is he now?"

The vampire rocked silently.

"Edgar, you know what I can do, now where is he?"

Will allowed a few more moments of silence to pass before he said, "Let that be one small sign of your misplaced arrogance."

"Nonsense – he has been unhinged by the evening's events, but . . ."

Edgar looked up at Will and said, "William of Mercia, I have dreamt of this day. I was a nobleman too, though you would hardly believe it to see me now." If he hadn't been so astonished, Will would have contradicted him because he was lucid and clear-eyed now and looked strong. "He is right in that I can tell you little – my role was merely . . . What does it matter. I ask only this: do for me what you did for them."

Will shook his head. "There has been too much killing here already."

"You would take nothing from me that he has not already stolen." He looked urgently at Will. "Burn this house, burn it from the cellars to the timbers and he will be weakened."

Wyndham shouted, "Edgar, silence!"

Something happened and Edgar winced and held his head, letting out a little yelp before saying, "His power rests in the objects he has here as much as in his knowledge, I am certain of it. Burn it all."

"Edgar!"

Edgar screamed and held his skull. Whatever punishment Wyndham was inflicting he was doing it remotely, and Will couldn't help but think of the similarity with the way Elfleda had punished Asmund for disobeying her. It was as if Wyndham had become more than a little like the creatures he detested so violently.

"Lorcan Labraid, Edgar, where can I find Lorcan Labraid? How can I reach him?"

Edgar clenched his teeth together, screaming and holding his skull.

"You have been there, you know it. You know the place. You have been there." He seemed in terrible agony, struggling to think more than one word at once.

Will said, "The gate is blocked, Edgar. I need a new gateway."

He was still holding his head with his hands, but he shook it, saying, "No, you have been there, you know it . . ." He let out a piercing scream.

Will heard Eloise say, "Oh God, Will, you have to do something for him."

"We'll take him away from here, beyond Wyndham's power." Even as he said it, he thought through the implications, knowing that Edgar too would need blood.

Wyndham laughed again, saying, "Nothing is beyond my power."

"It is true," said Edgar between his stifled screams. "It's inside me. Please . . ." He screamed again, clutching his skull as if he would tear it apart himself if he could.

Suddenly Edgar stood, rising to his full height before stepping out of the cage and collapsing on his knees in front of Will. He pulled his shirt apart with both hands, exposing his neck, and looked up at Will. "Burn this house!"

He screamed again, tearing his shirt and screwing his eyes closed. Through gritted teeth, he said, "Please, I beg of you, allow me to follow my queen." He kept his teeth clenched as he tried to stifle the scream that followed.

Will waited no longer, removing Edgar's head, closing his eyes against the light that burst out of him. Even with his eyes closed, the blue flashed inside them, and he heard the sound of something small falling to the floor.

When he opened his eyes again, he looked, but Eloise had seen it fall and was first to reach down and pick it up. She held it up for Will to see. He had no idea what it was until she explained.

"It's some sort of electronic chip – Wyndham must have implanted it in Edgar's skull – that's how he managed to inflict pain on him like that."

The sound of slow clapping emerged from the apparition and he said, "Well done, little girl, you've learned one of my secrets, but don't allow Edgar to trick you into thinking I rely on technology alone."

"I don't doubt it," said Will. "You raise the dead, you who call me evil."

"I raise the dead for the sake of good! And have they not come willingly? Yes, because they know what you are."

"What is it to you, who I am? Tell me that, Mr Wyndham, what is the nature of your personal vendetta against me?"

Wyndham smiled, full of malice, as he said, "I could

tell you, but I won't because I see it bothers you and that pleases me."

Will nodded, looking around the room, at the position of the lifelike apparition, at the walls and ceiling, then said, "So you can see us now, Mr Wyndham?"

"That I can."

"Then observe me well because the next time you see this face will be when I kill you. Now look upon your house for the last time."

Spotlights flashed on around the room, but Will simply took out his dark glasses and put them on. If anything, Eloise probably winced more than he did with the sudden brightness.

Wyndham's apparition sounded confident as it said, "It would be a mistake to follow Edgar's advice. For one thing . . ."

Will turned and threw his sword at a small box fitted to the wall above the door where they'd entered. It sparked and fused and the apparition disappeared.

He turned to Eloise and said, "We'll do as Edgar said."

She nodded. "We can't leave Marcus in here though – I can't bear the thought of him being burned as well."

"I'll carry him outside."

"I'll find something to light the fires."

"You're sure you feel well enough?"

She nodded, though he could tell from her movements

that she was still tender. He could tell too that she needed to be doing something, that the psychological wounds of this night would take longer to heal than the physical.

He picked up Marcus's body and carried him out, up the stairs and through the main hall. He carried him outside, a little distance from the house, on what he thought might be the drive, and laid him down in the snow. It was still falling heavily and Will feared it would cover the body before it was found.

He stood for a moment, but was distracted by a sound he recognised. He looked to his left and the three guard dogs were trotting towards them through the snow. There was no attack in them and when they came close, they edged round Will, still nervous of him. Then they lay in the snow, one near Marcus's head, the others at either arm, facing outwards as if guarding the body.

Will took a step back, but the dogs did not stir, and he looked at the odd cruciform shape they made with Marcus's body at the centre. And he could not help but think again of the skull in the ossuary at Marland. For here in front of him, though his life had denied it till the very end, was a true warrior.

When Will got back to the house, he called for a taxi and, despite the earlier driver's doubts about the weather, it was agreed instantly. He was about to head back down the cellar steps when Eloise called out, "Will, I'm in here."

He walked through into a drawing room where she had made a small bonfire of possessions, various small pieces of furniture stacked round a curtain she'd pulled from the windows. She was pouring liquid from a bottle on to the pyre.

"Formaldehyde. There's another bottle on the table there, and two more at the top of the cellar steps. I think enough got spilt in the cellar already without us worrying about that."

Will nodded and carried one of the bottles into the next room, a library and study. As much as it pained him to destroy books, he doused the shelves with the liquid, then carried the second bottle through to the dining room on the other side of the hall as Eloise walked off to find the kitchen.

He could hear her busily doing something, opening drawers, smashing glass, as he soaked the furnishings and the curtains, and could still hear her as he took the remaining two bottles and smashed them in the upstairs rooms.

When he came back down, she was in the hall with three wine bottles, each with a piece of ripped cloth stuffed into the neck. She held a box of matches.

"One for the cellar, one for the library, one for the

bonfire in the drawing room." She looked momentarily lost, but said, "The rest should take care of itself."

"I'll take the one for the cellar."

She shook her head. "I know you're not good with fire. I'll do them all."

Will didn't argue, but followed her down to the cellar. She lit the cloth in the end of the bottle and said, "Get ready to slam the door as soon as I throw this."

He nodded and she threw the bottle. Will slammed the door shut as the cellar went up in a percussive thud of flames. They ran up the stairs then and lit the two others, but this time Will insisted on taking one, much as the flames troubled him.

He threw it into the library and retreated, and as they reached the hall again, Eloise threw the last one at the makeshift bonfire in the drawing room. The pile of furniture was immediately swept with flames, shooting up towards the ceiling, licking at the walls. They watched for a moment then left.

Eloise stopped a little way from the house to look at Marcus, his features already lost beneath a thin white crust of snow, but his position marked by the dogs, which refused to move. They looked at Will as he passed, but were quite passive now.

And as Will and Eloise walked down the drive, Will thought of that bonfire she'd built in the drawing room and how, as it burned, it had reminded him of the pyre on which those women had been killed so long ago. Where were the witches now, he wondered. Why did they not come to advise and give comfort as they had done after Asmund's death?

But no spirits came and the two of them walked alone through the falling snow. When they reached the road, Will closed the gates again and tied the broken chain tight around them to slow the progress of any fire engine that came. The house was already glowing bright with flames in several of the windows.

They waited in silence for a while, and Eloise reached out and put her hand in his. Only as the taxi pulled in did Will say, "You should go to a hospital."

"I'm fine, really."

"Someone should look at you."

She looked at him and said, "OK, but not the hospital," and he understood who she meant.

The taxi driver lowered his window and said, "Blimey, is that place on fire?"

Will leaned in to give him his instructions.

30

Given the late hour, they went to the back door and knocked. They waited only a few seconds before Rachel appeared, her face becoming immediately wracked with concern and fear as she opened the door.

"Oh my God! What's happened?"

"I took a bit of a knock, that's all. Will wanted me to go to the hospital, but I'm fine, really I am."

"Come in, quickly." She ushered them in and brushed the snow off Eloise's coat, then turned without thinking and did the same for Will. "Where are you hurt?"

"Just my head, and my ribs maybe."

"OK, come upstairs, but I'm warning you, if it's beyond my first-aid skills, I'm calling a doctor." They headed out of the kitchen as Rachel said, "Make yourself comfortable, Will."

He walked through into the room with the sofas and bookshelves and sat down. He was there for some minutes before Chris emerged from his office, as if he'd only just become aware that they had visitors.

"Hello, Will! What brings this . . ."

"Eloise is hurt. Rachel's taking a look at her."

"Not seriously?"

Will shrugged and said, "We went to Wyndham's house." Chris appeared to be struggling to find the right response so Will continued, "He was keeping vampires imprisoned in his basement, some of them among those who were meant to help me, but they'd become so deranged with his tortures, it was pointless."

"So what happened to them?" He sat on the sofa opposite Will.

"All killed, as was a new friend of ours, and very nearly Eloise." He looked Chris in the eyes as he said, "Is it still so hard to believe this is the Wyndham you know?"

"Actually, yeah, it is, but . . . I guess Wyndham wasn't there." Will shook his head. "So you wasted your time."

"Oh, it was no victory for me, but it was most certainly a defeat for Wyndham. We destroyed the vampires he'd captured and Wyndham's house will by now have been razed to the ground."

As he said the words, Will saw the irony in them. They had wiped out a nest of vampires and destroyed it in flames – could Wyndham not see that his hateful pursuit had turned things upside down, to the extent that their roles were now reversed?

He heard Rachel and Eloise making their way back

down as Chris said, "Then at least you struck a blow against him, even if it was at a heavy cost." His thoughts appeared to be racing, his eyes jumping about, and he added, "A shame though, that you didn't find out anything from the vampires before you killed them, but if they were deranged like you say . . ."

Will said, "The frustration is no less than it was with Asmund, that none of these creatures seem capable of telling me what I must know, but I've come to understand that we are told things even when we think we are not." Chris offered a weak smile, confused. "I learned a great deal this evening."

Rachel and Eloise came into the room and Rachel said, "She's made of tough stuff, this one – I don't think there's any lasting damage." She looked sternly at Eloise though, and said, "But remember, if you have any of the symptoms I mentioned, it's straight to the hospital."

Eloise nodded and said, "Thanks, for everything," and gave Rachel a hug.

As she pulled away again, Rachel said, "I'll make you some tea, or do you want to get back to school?"

Eloise threw a glance at Will who understood immediately and said, "I think Eloise could use some tea, but we won't be going back to the school. We'll be staying in the city for a few days."

They remained only half an hour longer, the

conversation trailing over the same ground already covered by Will and Chris. Rachel's questions and concerns prevented Chris asking anything further.

And when they left, the city streets were deep with snow, though it had finally stopped falling. They walked to the church through the hollow air, immune to the beauty of it, lost in silence and in thoughts they both shared.

When they entered at the side door, Eloise said, "Do you mind if I have a moment?" She looked towards the altar.

"Not at all."

He walked along the nave with her, but she turned off into the Lady Chapel where she knelt, head bowed in her own private prayer. Will stayed some distance away. He thought he heard her weeping quietly at one point, but when she arose, her eyes were dry and she looked stronger.

They descended to the crypt and from there to his chambers, and once he'd lit the candles, they lay together on the daybed. She held on to him and leaned her head against his chest. Will put his arm round her shoulder in return and idly stroked her hair. For all that had happened this evening, these recent days, to be with her and hold her was enough to give him some peace.

They lay like that for a long time, until finally Eloise spoke, her voice hushed as she said, "What did you learn?"

"I'm sorry?"

"Earlier, you told Chris you'd learned a lot tonight."

"Less than I would have liked, and though we have dealt Wyndham some sort of blow, I fear there's so much more he can do. I said that in part because I have little doubt that Chris will tell Wyndham."

Eloise didn't question his logic this time, but said hopefully, "But you did learn something?"

"I learned from Edgar that we are close to Lorcan Labraid, though perhaps he did not know that the labyrinth is now impassable." He thought back to noble Edgar, the only one among those creatures he wished he could have spared, and to the words they'd exchanged. "Of course, I told him that, and yet he remained insistent, so perhaps he refers to some other place, or some other way of gaining entrance to the gateway."

"If only you'd learned as much from the queen."

"I learned something more precious from the queen, something that offers both more hope and also more danger for you."

Eloise looked up at him before lowering her head back to his chest as she said, "What?"

"I need you, you need me, Jex said so, the medallion

said so, the witches believe it, yet both Asmund and Elfleda tried to kill you."

"Only because they were so desperate for blood."

"Possibly, and yet their whole existence was apparently aimed at fulfilling my destiny. But more, when I told Elfleda that you were the girl spoken of in the prophecies, she said, 'Don't you think I know that,' before trying to feed from you. Why would someone who had endured so much to fulfil my destiny, to see the prophecies realised, *why* would she respond in such a way to learning your identity?"

Will had already had time to consider it, but he was impressed that within a few seconds, Eloise turned, leaning with both hands on his chest, looking into his eyes as she said, "Because the prophecies conflict! Because you have two possible destinies! She tried to kill me because you need me to help you reach that other destiny, the one that frees you from Lorcan Labraid."

She looked joyful for a moment, then hopeful, then a little less so as she accepted there was more hope than fact in this. She moved back into her previous position, putting her head back on Will's chest.

"Everyone wants to kill me," she said.

"I don't," said Will, stroking her hair again now that she was settled.

"No, you don't." She was silent for a little while, then said, "I wish we could stay here forever."

"Me too."

He thought of the city far above, covered with snow, and imagined that snow never melting, the world falling into an enchantment that would not be broken. For so many centuries he'd despaired of being trapped in this body forever, in these chambers, yet right at this moment, he could think of no better fate.

31

This is not the end, far from it. This is the beginning. I never imagined it would be easy, that there would not be casualties. And I cannot deny that my thoughts and emotions are conflicted by the turn of events.

This is evil I am facing, I have no doubt of it, but is the battle worth the cost? I don't know. I continue only in the knowledge that good must always triumph over evil, no matter what price we pay for that victory. If I surrender now, how can I know what terrors will be visited upon the world?

But the losses! It seems he betrayed me, Marcus Jenkins, or rather that I misread his character or underestimated my enemy's powers of persuasion. Yet he was brave, I'll give him that, and honourable, and would have made a fine gentleman if given the chance. What future he would have had where he grew up, I don't know, but that makes it no easier to accept his death, a death I lured him to with empty promises of a brighter future.

If there's a greater conflict within me than that surrounding the death of young Marcus, it's my feelings regarding William of Mercia himself. Perhaps I'm confused only because it's the first time I've seen him in the flesh, so to speak, the person my entire life has been dedicated to destroying, even before I knew it.

When I saw him, it was within the context of battle and yet still he seemed somehow more decent, more honourable, more . . . human than I had imagined. His love for the girl is plain for anyone to see. And as shocked as I was by the ferocity with which he killed the vampire queen, I am certain he was driven by the fury of seeing her murder Marcus.

I have witnessed a humanity of sorts in these creatures before, most notably in Baal, but William of Mercia behaved in a way that almost fills me with admiration. Almost, but not quite.

It was impossible too for me to fail to observe that he was a handsome boy, tall and charismatic, and I cannot but wonder at my mother's fixation with him. Did the young Arabella Harriman fall in love with this demon? And was the shock of seeing him so many years later born as much out of those impassioned, adolescent feelings as from the impact of seeing him unchanged?

Has the course of my entire life been determined by the fact that my mother's first love failed to grow old?

If that is the case, how appropriate that she should inadvertently confer the same wretched fate on her own child.

You may wonder that I speak as if cursed, but at this moment, I wonder if I was, if by appearing beside my mother's carriage that night, William of Mercia handed me the curse of being his arch-enemy.

Is it not a curse to lose the world in which you belong? Yes, I have adapted, in my language and my dress and my customs. I pass for a modern man more readily than these demons could ever manage to do, so much so that I would now be a stranger if returned to my own time. But the world I knew and belonged to has disappeared, and no matter how long you live, you are always tied in your heart to the time of your youth.

I became an alchemist, yet the real alchemy is that which already lies within us, that makes us live and love and grow old, a magic we hand on to our children and they to theirs. I thought my alchemy had stopped time, but time continued relentlessly and merely left me behind. Yes, a part of me is locked eternally in the summer of 1753, the sports and the pastimes, the society of my family and its connections, the pretty smile of Lady Maria Dangrave.

That is why I cannot stop, because nothing can get me back to the summer of 1753 and that smile. My mother's experiment cast me ashore here, in this distant future, and I was sent here to destroy the evil that is carried within the person of William of Mercia.

I'll grant the possibility that he does not know the evil he carries within, that he is merely a vessel, but he carries it nevertheless, and even if it is my last act, you have to understand that I have no choice but to destroy him. If you had seen the same things as I have, understood them as I have, I assure you that you would feel the same.

32

The sun had been shining all day and the snow, deep as it lay, was thawing quickly. After weeks of bone-jarring cold, milder weather was promised, together with the hope that the worst of the winter might be behind them.

From the back of the car, Chris looked out at fields that still glowed white in the twilight and the part of him that was still young felt saddened that it would have all melted within a day or two. For weeks to come the world would probably look damp and dreary.

"Be glad when this has all gone," said Field. "Seen enough snow for one year, don't you think?"

Chris looked at him, head shaved, tattoos creeping up from beneath his collar as if they were slowly growing up his neck. Field was solidly built, but carried another whole body's worth of padding. Apart from the possible uses of his doorman's bulk, Chris couldn't quite understand what Field was doing with them.

They turned into the school gates and Chris started to

tap his foot without realising he was doing it, a sudden release of nervous energy.

Wyndham picked up on it straight away and said, "Relax, Christopher, they're in the city, you know they are, so there's no one to see us, no one to hinder our progress."

Field laughed, then looked at Chris with a puzzled expression for a moment before saying, "I know where I know you from! Don't you run that hippy veggie-burger type place?"

Wyndham laughed, saying, "Mr Field, you are a tease."

Field smiled, pleased with himself, completely unaware that he'd just been silenced. And then the car stopped and they climbed out, waiting only while the driver handed Wyndham a long cardboard box. Chris knew, of course, that it contained a sword.

Dr Higson met them in the hall and ushered them immediately towards the chapel. Chris noticed the headmaster's hand was heavily bandaged, which filled him with misgivings, but Field, suddenly useful, allayed them by asking Higson outright.

"What happened to your hand, Doc?"

Higson grimaced at the way he'd been addressed, but lifted the hand up to display the bandaging as he said, "I run the perimeter of the school every morning, but the ground's frozen of course, which I didn't allow for. Took a tumble, bruised the wrist, broke some fingers."

Field produced an odd superior laugh as though the injury supported one of his long-held beliefs, then said, "I've never held with jogging."

No one replied.

They stepped down into the chapel and Higson waited until the door was closed before saying, "Please, follow me."

There were some steps to a crypt towards the left-hand side of the altar, but Higson led them instead to the right where, behind the altar, there was a small locked room that looked as if it had once been used for storage. It was empty now except for some electric camping lanterns in one corner.

Once inside, Higson locked the door, then opened a panel in one of the walls. There was another locked door beyond it, but before opening that, Higson reached down and picked up one of the lanterns, saying, "We'll all need one of these."

They picked them up and turned them on, then Higson unlocked the door and started down the steps on the other side of it. Before following, Wyndham turned to Chris and Field and said, "Very few people know about this tunnel, but trust me, this is not what we have come to see."

They descended, and at the bottom of the steps they

followed a narrow tunnel for some distance until it opened into a small circular chamber. Chris moved around the walls, but could find nothing to suggest any further openings.

Field looked up at the roof of the chamber and said, "What is it, a priest-hole or something?"

Wyndham smiled and said, "It's a gateway to another world, Mr Field, something quite extraordinary."

Field said, "What d'you reckon, Tofu, you just looked around the walls, see any gateway?"

It took a moment for Chris to realise Field was talking to him, and he laughed and said, "No, as it happens, I don't, but I've known Phillip long enough not to doubt him."

"Quite," said Wyndham. "You see, Mr Field, this gateway is designed to be opened by one person and one person alone. So though I knew it was here, I had no way of accessing it. Then Christopher suggested something, and I have to admit I was sceptical, but he convinced me, and I'm glad he did . . ." He opened the box and removed the weapon. "A sabre, used by William of Mercia himself, touched by him, if you will. Now stand back and behold."

Higson immediately stood with his back to the wall. Chris and Field followed suit and then Wyndham drove the point of the sword into the floor of the chamber. It was stone, and yet the blade slid through and the sabre stood upright when Wyndham let go and joined the others at the edge of the chamber.

The ground startled to tremble. Chris put his hand flat against the wall and realised that, despite the cold, his palm was damp. He could feel his heart racing too as the ground in front of him appeared to wobble and shimmer, then it peeled apart around the impaled sword, revealing a spiralling stone staircase descending into darkness.

They all stood in silence at first, matching the hollow stillness that now surrounded them. Unsurprisingly, it was Field who spoke first, laughing as he said, "Now *that* is amazing."

Wyndham appeared to appreciate the comment, but still said, "On the contrary, Mr Field, *that* is just the beginning. Come, follow me."

They set off down the steps, and on reaching the bottom, set off along another tunnel. But there was no longer a single tunnel, and they turned several times, but also ignored many other tunnels that led off the route they followed.

At first, Chris tried to remember the turnings they'd taken, in case he became separated, but he lost track, not least because he was more spooked by the atmosphere down here than he cared for the others to know. There was something sinister in the air of the place. Perhaps it was just because of the other tunnels and the air moving between them, but there seemed a constant background noise, sometimes like wind howling through distant chambers, other times like the whispering of many voices.

Was this the underworld, he wondered, or at least the entrance to it? There was something malign in the atmosphere, there was no doubting that, and he imagined being alone down here would unsettle a person's mind very quickly.

They walked for some considerable time, until finally Chris detected that they were walking up a long, slight gradient. The thought that they were heading back towards the surface, however slowly, gave him some reassurance.

And then, quite unexpectedly, they stepped into a large round chamber with a domed roof above them, entrances to another two passages on the other side of it.

Speaking quietly, Wyndham said, "Place your lanterns around the room, avoiding the centre of course."

Only as he added the final instruction did Chris realise there was something in the centre of the room, a sight that so astounded him he almost dropped his lantern, and struggled to tear his eyes away as he placed it on the floor.

The body of a man hung by his feet from the roof.

Chris couldn't see what the binding was, but it also bound his legs together and his arms to his sides. It looked almost as though roots growing down from the earth above had been used to fasten him in place. And as if that wasn't enough, a wooden stake had been driven into his heart.

His clothes appeared to be leather, but had taken on almost the same colour as his mummified skin which clung to his bone structure, making him look barely human. Yet he had been human at some point, and the remains of black hair hung from his head and showed on his withered face where there had once been a beard.

Beneath his head, in a pile on the floor, lay discarded swords, as if some sort of offering, or perhaps even as a mockery to the man – or creature – whose slow death must have been one long torture. Free yourself, the swords seemed to be saying, reach out for one of us and free yourself.

"Gentlemen," said Wyndham with the theatricality of a circus ringmaster, "behold Lorcan Labraid, the Suspended King of legend, the last of the four, the only one who yet lives."

"Except for one slight fly in the ointment," said Field. "This guy's dead, and he's been dead for a pretty long time by the look of him."

Even as Field spoke, Chris realised with horror that

the creature had opened its eyes, first at the sound of Wyndham's voice, then looking to Field. Field must have seen it himself because before Wyndham could reply he said, "Good God, I don't believe it, he's staring at me, the ugly . . ."

"Quite," said Wyndham.

Higson stood back almost near the tunnel entrance, as if wanting no further part in the proceedings. But then Chris guessed he'd seen the creature before. For his own part, Chris couldn't resist moving a little closer.

He was amazed that a creature he'd heard spoken of in such revered tones – the evil of the world, who called to William of Mercia, the Suspended King – could look so diminished, so pathetic. And yet there was something disturbing about him still and Chris went to great efforts to avoid his gaze, even as he was aware of it following him round the room.

"Well, Christopher, tell me what you're thinking."

He turned to Wyndham and said, "I'm thinking so many things, but I suppose the most obvious is, doesn't this finish it? Kill Lorcan Labraid and it's all over for Will. OK, you'd still have to kill him, but he'd be stopped from ever fulfilling his destiny."

He felt a twinge of guilt as he spoke, but as always at times like this, he reminded himself that he owed no loyalty to Will. As he and Rachel had stood paralysed in the church at Puckhurst, he'd heard Will bartering their blood against Eloise's, and if Asmund had accepted, he would no doubt have given them up. No, he owed no loyalty to William of Mercia.

"That's very true," said Wyndham. "And naturally I've considered it, but as ill-equipped as Labraid seems to defend himself, there is some sort of protective force in place around him, one which no sword has yet managed to penetrate." He gestured to the floor beneath Lorcan Labraid's head. "You witness the swords of those who have tried."

Field had been walking in a slow circle round the suspended body, but said now, "No one's hit it hard enough, that's all. I don't care what it's made of, you hit something hard enough, it'll break."

Wyndham shrugged and said, "I'm all for another attempt, if you think you can bring your considerable strength to bear, Mr Field."

"Well, I don't see Tofu or the Doc being up to it." He looked at the pile of swords on the floor, edged closer and kicked them. A few skittered clear and he examined them before picking up a broadsword. He gripped it with both hands, giving some less than convincing swipes through the air before approaching the hanging figure.

"Gotta sever the head, right?"

"That's correct."

321

With no more ceremony, Field took a big swing and the sword swooped down and hit the side of Lorcan Labraid's neck. Chris prepared himself for what he expected to follow, the brief slicing of flesh before the explosion of blue light. But as Wyndham had suggested, the sword blade bounced off as if Field had just met rock or metal.

"Whoa!" Field struggled to stay on his feet from the power of the rebound and the sword flew from his hands and hit the wall at the side of the room. Labraid appeared unmoved, his eyes still passively following his observers.

"OK, see your point, but this can be done. Where did the sword go?"

Chris looked at him and said, "You're bleeding." There was a spot of blood on Field's cheek and Chris pointed to his own cheek to show him where.

Field reached up and wiped it, looking at his fingers as he said, "I don't know how I did that. Mind, it took it out of me, that did."

Chris looked back at him, but could no longer speak because Field's face was now bleeding in several places at once, the blood oozing not from wounds, but out of the skin itself, then out of his eyes.

"I'm not feeling too special," said Field, still unaware of what was happening to him. His face was running with blood now and it was soaking through his clothes from his body, and then Field let out a dull, surprised scream, and the blood flew away from him, like iron filings to a magnet, a red mist which settled and clung instantly to Lorcan Labraid.

Field stood for a moment, chalk white, stunned, and collapsed into dust which billowed across the floor of the chamber, leaving nothing, not an item of clothing, not a watch or piece of jewellery.

The sword, which had been across the room, and the other swords that Field had kicked aside, slid back across the floor and settled in the position they'd been in before. Chris heard Wyndham laugh at this development, suggesting he'd expected Field's death, had almost certainly brought him along for that purpose alone, but not for the swords to rearrange themselves.

But then even Wyndham fell silent. Within seconds of the blood mist being absorbed, a visible transformation started to take place in Lorcan Labraid.

His flesh, which had been leathery and mummified, filled out and regained the texture and colour of skin. The body filled out too, straining against its bindings. Even the clothes seemed restored. His hair, which had looked like mere remnants, now hung dark and long from his head, and grew again into a beard on his face.

Within a matter of seconds, and despite the stake

through his chest and the bindings that kept him suspended, Lorcan Labraid had come to look very much alive. Chris found himself stepping backwards, doubting the stake would be enough to contain a man who looked this fierce, this strong.

Chris heard Higson say in a small voice, "I didn't expect that."

Wyndham was exuberant as he said, "You see, Christopher, you see the true evil we face."

Labraid's mouth opened, revealing his fangs, and then his voice, effortlessly powerful.

"Who are you to be here?"

"I am Phillip Wyndham and now, Lorcan Labraid, whether you like it or not, you are at my disposal."

Labraid laughed and said, "You? You are nothing. You speak of evil? With what knowledge?" Wyndham seemed unsettled, the first time Chris had seen him like that. And then Labraid laughed again and said playfully, "Can you run?"

There was no time for answers. The four lanterns exploded and died, plunging the room into pitch-darkness. And immediately from one of the other passageways came a furious screaming, not of someone in pain, but of some creature – or creatures because it sounded as if there were many of them – bent on bloodshed.

"Quick!" shouted Wyndham. "Follow me!"

Chris responded instantly, tearing into the darkness, finding the tunnel entrance with his outstretched hands, bumping into Higson as he too struggled to escape. Wyndham shouted back to them and they ran on.

Higson had got into the tunnel first, which meant Chris was at the back, that he would be caught first. That only intensified his terror, almost robbing his legs of the ability to move, like those nightmares he'd had as a child, being chased by witches or monsters, his legs like lead.

But Chris kept running into the blackness, blind, judging his direction from his outstretched hands and the sound of footfalls ahead of him and the terrifying screams behind and the occasional shouts of Wyndham.

Wyndham sounded confident, even triumphant, but Chris was too riddled with fear to share in that confidence. The screams were still distant, but they gained on them in leaps, and Chris didn't know how far they had left to run or at which point they would reach safety.

He ran on, and thought of what had happened to Field and of the transformation of Lorcan Labraid. He thought of the way the lanterns had exploded and the screams that pursued them now, not even wanting to think what creatures might be making a noise like that.

For the first time, he thought he understood the true meaning of evil, and for the first time, he wondered if Wyndham himself really understood it, or the nature of the evil he had just unleashed.

Acknowledgements

Thanks go to the following people. To Sarah Molloy and all at AM Heath. To Stella Paskins and Elizabeth Law, and all at Egmont in the UK and US respectively. To Jane Tait for her expert attention to detail. To Sharon Chai for her vision. To Una, as before. And finally, thanks to the many people who've contacted me in the last year to tell my how much they enjoyed *Blood*, both new readers and old friends, with a special mention to Helen P, who perhaps knew before anyone that I would write these books . . .

> *"Bliss was it in that dawn to be alive,*
> *But to be young was very heaven!"*

Coming soon

death

BOOK THREE OF THE MERCIAN TRILOGY

ELECTRIC MONKEY

To find out more about other fantastic books
for young adult readers check out the brilliant new
ELECTRIC MONKEY website:

Trailers

Blogs

News and Reviews

Competitions

Downloads

Free stuff

Author interviews

 Like us on Facebook

 Follow us on Twitter

www.electricmonkeybooks.co.uk